Last Man Out

A Markos Mystery
Book one

Isabella Adams

Solstice Publishing - www.solsticepublishing.com

Last Man Out

Isabella Adams

Dedication

For my dream pathway: my pons, thalamus, and cerebral cortex. Without my dreams, my nightly forays into other worlds and realms, my writing would have no life. Please, Cortex, keep up the good work.

Chapter One

Tony had not expected this.

He had not expected Ross to fight back. He knew that it was risky killing Ross in a cave, but it had to be done. Ross was always such a loudmouth. He always had something to say—about everything. Tony thought that he would keep this secret though. He thought that Ross knew what was at stake. But Tony was wrong. Who knew the pretentious little shit had a conscience? As far as Tony could tell, Ross was always too busy being an ignorant know-it-all to worry about morality.

Physically, there was nothing extraordinary about Ross, either. He looked so benign, so average. He just looked like a little pussy. Tony only realized how much he had underestimated the rich little snot when he fought back. And this made Tony angry.

When it was time, Tony stopped his gentle movements through the water. In a cave, every action counts. If Tony was too powerful, clouds of thick sediment billowed into the water and obscured his vision. No, in order to move through the water in a cave Tony used subtlety. He only had to swish his toes gently and he would glide along. Peaceful, content.

And so, Tony stopped, and everything was silent. The caves were always silent. That was the reason Tony yearned for his time underground. Down here, there was no noise. No cars. No people clamoring for more of what they thought they wanted. Down here, it was quiet. This was Tony's happy place. This was his domain.

But the time for subtlety and peace was gone.

Tony ripped the regulator out of Ross's mouth without a problem. Ross did what he was trained to do. He dipped his face down and reached for his lanyard, his spare regulator. It was supposed to be attached to his chest so he could breathe without using his hands if he needed to. Tony had taken care of that as well.

Ross's lips groped for the silicone mouthpiece, but it wasn't there. Tony had ripped it away, too.

Tony grabbed Ross's arms behind his back and held on tight. Ross thrashed. Tony tightened his grip. He felt Ross's shoulder pop out of place. Ross's flailing fins kicked up soft silt on the bottom of the cave floor, and Tony's vision was compromised.

This was not turning out as Tony had expected.

Tony squeezed Ross's arms closer together. But Ross kept fighting back.

God damn you! Tony thought.

The tunnel they were in was narrow and the clearance was low. Tony had prepared for a struggle, but this felt more difficult, more demanding. Maybe it was because Tony was killing someone for the first time. He had always heard that the first time was the toughest. Either way, the two of them, plus their gear, took up the whole section of cave that Tony chose for this purpose.

Here, there was a crevice where he could secure the body. People had been found dead here before. Here was perfect.

CRACK.

Tony felt his nose break as Ross threw his head back. White heat shot through to the back of Tony's skull. Although it had been an attempt to free himself, Ross's action only made Tony angrier.

Die already, you piece of shit!

Blood poured into Tony's mask. Bubbles formed as the red liquid surged into the small space. Still, Tony held Ross's arms tight. It wouldn't be long now.

Ross thrashed again. Tony could taste metallic liquid running down the back of his throat. He blew out hard through his regulator to try to clear his airway. Ross's fins churned up more silt, and what was left of Tony's visibility was gone. Blood stung his eyes and he closed his lids tight.

Just remember your training.

Somewhere in the back of his mind, Tony knew that his training was meant to help save lives, not end them. He pushed away any doubt about this being the right move. It had to be done.

Soon, Ross stopped fighting as hard. Soon, his body, covered in thousands of dollars of dive gear, went limp. Tony gave the dead body a rueful shove.

Bastard.

He took his mask off and spit out his regulator. He tasted dirt and blood against the back of his tongue. The silty water stung his nostrils, but with a firm blow, he cleared out enough blood to be able to see. Or at least he hoped so.

Tony hit the purge button on his regulator and replaced it in his mouth. In the small dark space, he methodically cleaned his mask and carefully placed it back on to his face. He tilted his head back and blew out, sealing the edge securely on his cheeks and forehead.

Tony felt around the limp body for Ross's regulator. He grabbed the brand-new silicone and rubber mouthpiece and shoved it in to Ross's water-filled mouth. Ross had always acted so superior to the other cave divers they knew. He always had to have the best gear, dive the best sites.

Gear didn't do shit for you now, did it? You smug little bitch.

Tony pushed the dead body deeper into the cave, making sure it was lodged firmly against the chosen fissure. It had to look like Ross had gotten stuck, panicked, and drowned. Once Tony felt confident about the body's position, he turned around and focused on finding his line markers. Soon he felt the plastic triangles stamped with his initials and followed them back out of the cave system. They went back to the cavern that led down into the miles and miles of tortuous tunnels that snaked their way under the entire state of Florida.

The water cleared as Tony moved further away from the kill site. His high-powered dive light cut through the darkness like high beams in a snowstorm. A white catfish squirmed across his cone of light and Tony jumped, hitting his head on the roof of the cave. Sediment fell down around him.

Dammit! It's just a fish.

Most people in Florida didn't even know this cave existed. Most people were unaware of the miles of secret passages that connected Florida's natural springs. But this was Tony's church, his quiet, peaceful paradise.

Once he could see the small area of light shining through the water high above him, Tony knew that he was out of the cave. He passed by the warning sign posted at the entrance to every known cave in Florida:

STOP
Prevent your death!
Go no further.
FACT: More than 300 divers, including open water scuba instructors, have died in caves just like this one.
FACT: You need training to dive. You need <u>cave training</u> and <u>cave equipment</u> to <u>cave dive</u>.
FACT: Without cave training and cave equipment, divers can die here.
FACT: It <u>CAN</u> happen to <u>YOU!</u>
THERE'S NOTHING IN THIS CAVE WORTH DYING FOR!
DO NOT GO BEYOND THIS POINT.

Tony chuckled at the irony. He sat silently at the bottom of the natural spring for a few moments, enjoying the comfort of the water. When he was ready, he pulled off his mask again. With vicious force, he smashed one of the lenses against his knee. The glass broke but didn't shatter.

Perfect.

He reached out his arm and dropped the beloved piece of gear. The plastic and glass, the window through which Tony had seen so much of heaven, swayed gently back and forth, as it fell slowly to the soft sand next to the sign. After a moment, he drew a deep breath through his regulator.

Damn, this is gonna hurt.

He kicked hard off of the ground. Like an untied balloon when let go, Tony shot up to the surface of the calm, innocent looking water.

Chapter Two

The Florida morning air was saturated with mist. Andromeda Markos pushed herself through the humidity, even though she felt like she was breathing in a cloud. She could taste the salt suspended in the morning fog. The mangroves nearby were rife with water birds indigenous to this area of the state. When she did not have her ear buds in, Andie occasionally heard the eerie cry of an osprey as it brought food back to its young, perched high on top of a telephone pole.

Her phone vibrated in her hand and a photo of her mother popped up on the screen.

If it's not one thing, it's your mother, Andie thought. She had to slow down to a trot while she answered.

"*Ela,* Mama," she answered in Greek. The high-pitched cackle of a red headed woodpecker sounded from nearby, chastising Andie for interrupting its breakfast.

"*Mehxehases!* I am old and alone, and you don't call. I could have fallen and you would never know. I could be dead. Are you out running again? Are you alone? Andromeda, you know better! There are men out there just waiting to take women and do horrible things to them."

"Ma, please. And about last night, I'm sorry, I forgot." Andie wanted to add a comment about her mother obviously not being dead, but she managed to hold her tongue.

She was supposed to have called her widowed mother back the night before. The truth is that she had not forgotten. She just didn't want to hear the lecture about living so close but not coming over enough. Andie was sure that even if she lived with her mother it wouldn't be enough. She also didn't want to answer more questions about why she and her ex-husband Pete were not living together, or why he didn't escort her on her morning runs.

"Ok, *hara mou*, I forgive you. So, are you and Petros coming for Sunday brunch?"

Andie had to stop running all together. The reminder of the obligatory weekly meal exhausted her energy. She pushed frizzy black curls out of her oval, olive toned face. She paused before answering; she drew in a lungful of the wet air in an attempt to calm herself. Andie stood on the Pinellas Trail at 6:13 AM catching her breath and trying not to yell at her seventy-five-year old mother. She turned to the wooded side of the trail and peered in between the leaves.

"I'm not having this conversation again, ma. We're divorced," she finally said. "And I have to finish my run and get back home. Kallie has to be at school in like an hour."

"*Keh Kaliope mou?*" Her mother's voice softened. She had a tender spot for her only granddaughter.

"How is she? She has a phone, ma. You can call her yourself." Andie instantly felt bad for snapping. Her mother lived alone in the same house Andie had grown up in, and what she needed was love and connection with her family, not impatience. "Sorry, mama. Look, if I promise to come by tonight, can I finish my run without having to hang up on you?"

Her mother made a tisk sound on the other end of the line.

"Always in such a hurry," her mother said. "*Ndakse, Andromeda mou, sagapo prosehe*, tonight. There are lots of crazy men out there who would grab you. I don't want to read about you in the paper."

"I love you too, mama, and I'll be careful, I promise."

Andie jabbed at the screen of her phone harder than necessary but the call didn't end. She got frustrated and had to hit it two more times before the signal finally dropped.

Gamoto, she thought. *If it's not one thing, it's your mother.*

Seventeen minutes later, Andie stepped through the sliding glass door into her dining room. She pulled it closed behind her and locked it. She stopped and closed her eyes, momentarily enraptured by the pure joy of air conditioning. She breathed in the cold, dry air and reflected that it somehow felt sharper, cleaner. Her brain wandered to the last time she changed the return vent filters and she made a mental note to add that to her never-ending to-do list.

Andie's two-year-old Great Dane, Athena, bound to her as she stood with her eyes closed. The gigantic dog leaned heavily against her sticky legs. Andie knew that she would have short, brindle colored hair stuck to her skin when she got into the shower.

Fall on the west coast of Florida can be Eden or Hades, it all depends on the day. On this particular day in October, Andie's morning run had not been ideal. The mist among the mangroves was beautiful. It shrouded the coast in quiet mystery, but it also meant that Andie had to run in 100% humidity. On days like this, there was no hope of staying dry. No sweat would evaporate, ever; it had no place to go. So, her long hair and her running clothes were soaking wet as she basked in the glorious cold of her dining room.

"Mom?" Kallie's voice held the questioning disdain of teenagerhood. "What are you doing?"

Andie looked over at her daughter sitting at the dining table nearby. She had her journal in front of her as she ate breakfast. Andie felt Athena start to lick the drying sweat off of her legs.

"I see you're not ready yet," Andie said. She moved to the living room and collapsed on the floor under the ceiling fan.

"Nope," Kallie answered with a mouth full of cereal.

Andie spread her arms out to her side and enjoyed the gentle movement of air around her. Her skin started to itch where the sweat was drying. She closed her eyes again and tried to pull together enough energy to shower and get ready for work. *Thank God it's Friday*, she thought.

"Is your stuff ready for the weekend at least?" she asked from the ground. There was no answer. Andie raised her head and looked towards the dining room. Kallie was still there, eating her Cheerios. ®

"Hello?" Andie said. "Is your stuff ready for your weekend with your dad?" She added an edge to her voice. Andie felt that with teenagers you sometimes had to stoop to their level.

Kallie rolled her eyes. "Yes!" she said. "Stop asking, ok?"

Andie laughed and dropped her head back onto the bamboo laminate. "Ouch," she said under her breath. She hit the floor harder than she had intended.

"Someone is extra teenaged this morning," Andie said louder. She could almost hear the eye-roll from where she lay.

She groaned as she pulled herself up and walked to her daughter. Andie loved to run, but some days running did not love her back. She knew that lying under cold, moving air after a run wasn't going to help her muscles recover any faster, but jumping right into a hot shower without cooling down wasn't a great option either.

"It's just that you asked me like sixteen times," Kallie grumped.

"And you, *kore mou*, answered me only once."

Andie wrapped her arms around her only child. Kallie had inherited Andie's average height, but she was developing the same voluptuous curves that Pete's mother had. She easily could have been a model for the ancient Greek statues Andie's mother kept around her house. In spite of Kallie's protestations, Andie squeezed her tight.

"Aggg, gross! Mom, your clothes are disgusting, get away!"

Andie pulled away, but not before planting a salty kiss on Kallie's forehead.

"Ok, enough with that. Watch your attitude. And seriously, get yourself and your stuff for the weekend ready by the time I'm out of the shower. We're leaving in twenty minutes."

On most days, Dr. Andromeda Markos started seeing patients at 8:30. On this particular Friday, however, she had agreed to come in early to accommodate a new patient. As she got into the shower, she had no way of knowing that this new patient held a dark secret. Or that this secret would someday soon put her life in danger.

Chapter Three

"He says he put Vicks on it and now it burns worse than before."

Andie's Medical Assistant, Stella, called her before she reached the office. Markos Family Medicine had patients of all ages, but being in Florida, there was a high percentage of older people who came to the office for care. Word eventually got around that Andie spoke Greek, and her patient population quickly became overwhelmingly Greek-speaking, and overwhelmingly geriatric.

Andie rubbed her eyes. It was going to be a long Friday.

"Ok, have him come in to see the wound care nurse. And tell him that menthol and diabetic foot ulcers don't mix," she said. "I'm almost there."

As she ended the call with Stella, the phone rang again.

"Maria! *¿Como esta, Querida?*" Andie said.

"*Ay mi Madre.* The baby is sick, so I'm not sure I'll make it to breakfast tomorrow, I'm sorry."

Since Andie returned to Tarpon Springs after medical school, she and three of her childhood best friends had been meeting every Saturday at the same restaurant for breakfast. Occasionally, something interrupted the ritual— vacationn, childbirth, a wedding—but not even her divorce or being on-call had kept her from the standing date.

"Come on mama, Juany can take care of her," Andie replied.

Maria was a middle school teacher. She was the most responsible of the four friends. She also was Cuban-

American, which meant that, like Andie, her life was dictated to a large degree by her culture.

Maria sighed on the other end of the line. Andie heard a baby whimpering nearby.

"Whatever you need honey," Andie said more gently. "Can I do anything to help?"

"*Gracias mamí*, but no. You know what, pray for healing, ok?" Maria made a shushing sound as she attempted to soothe her ill child.

"Will do," Andie said. "I hope she feels better, and I hope we see you tomorrow. *Cuídate querida.*"

"*Igual mamí.*"

Andie walked through the back door of her office a few moments later and grabbed a cup of Bustello coffee before heading to her office.

"*Gracias Lupé!*" she called down the hall. The front desk girl routinely spoiled her by having espresso ready when she arrived every morning.

"*Claro que si, Doctora,*" she heard in return.

Andie rushed behind her desk and dropped her bag into the large drawer that was supposed to hold files. Stella followed her and stood waiting.

"Hey Stella, good morning. How's Mr. Papadopoulos?"

"He'll be here this morning sometime. He says he'll try not to use the Vicks any more on his ulcers."

"Yeah, he said that last time, too." Andie pulled on her white coat as Stella handed her the papers she had been holding.

"Is this the new patient?" She looked down at the intake form. "Follow up from hyperbaric treatment, seriously?"

Stella shrugged. "I guess there was a diving accident and he had to go to a decompression chamber." Her voice dropped, "He says that his dive partner *died* in the cave. He says that he got so freaked out that he lost his mask and just swam up towards the light, ended up with decompression sickness. It's a good thing he was able to call for help."

Andie looked at the paperwork again. No known allergies; history of sinus surgery; allergy medicine and nasal spray daily, and Sudafed as needed. Yup, definitely a SCUBA diver.

Andie's ex-husband, Pete, was a Technical Diver. He owned a small dive shop near the Sponge Docks in downtown Tarpon Springs, the small town in which Andie was born and raised. Pete's place was a hole in the wall, really, but he loved it. Actually, he loved it so much that it was one of the reasons they were now divorced. Civilly divorced, that is.

In the eyes of The Greek Orthodox Church, and Andie's mother, they were still married. The Church did not recognize the legal rulings of the State of Florida. So, every Sunday, Andie, Pete, and Kallie went to Sunday mass with her mother. They all sat together and pretended to be a good, little, intact family. Andie did her best not to bicker with her cheating ex while in church. Some days she was more successful than others.

Andie sighed. She was a certified cave diver as well, and while she was a Family Practitioner by training, she specialized in dive medicine. Any time a diver was injured, or needed to follow up after decompression treatment, they came to Andie. Some days she regretted this choice. It only reminded her of younger, more foolish days.

"Is he nice?" she asked Stella. Stella shrugged again.

"He seemed ok, a little jumpy. Kinda gave me the creeps, but whatever. His pressure and pulse were up a bit—you know, first visit and all."

Andie looked at the vitals. *He's young, so let's hope it's just White Coat Syndrome and nothing to do with his decompression sickness*, she thought.

When she walked in to the room, she changed her opinion; something about him told her his abnormal vital signs had nothing to do with being at a new doctor's office. And she doubted it had anything to do with his recent episode of decompression sickness, or "the bends," either. The man who greeted her stood up and shook her hand. His palm was sweaty and he was shaking. He looked her in the eyes, and instantly Andie was suspicious.

"Mr. Anthony Siegel?" she said as they completed their greeting. "I'm Dr. Markos."

"Yeah, Tony, um, everyone calls me Tony."

***

After work, Andie drove to the Sponge Docks to drop Kallie off at her father's shop. The smell of stale cigarette smoke and neoprene greeted her as she stepped into the dark, cluttered store.

"There's my girls!" Pete moved out from behind the cash register where he was closing out for the night. He hugged Kallie and attempted to kiss Andie.

"Don't even think about it," she said. She held her arm out straight, her palm stiff against his chest.

"Aww, *moro mou*, so hostile." His dark eyes were accusatory as he walked back to his piles of credit card receipts and cash. He pulled his shirt collar away from his neck, exposing a jungle of curly, graying hair bursting to escape. He continued with his accounting.

The last thing Andie wanted to do was engage in any unnecessary conversation with her ex-husband, but she knew that Pete would know about the dive accident. Her desire to know more about her patient won out against her hatred of talking to Pete. She casually asked if he had heard anything about any incidents recently.

"Why do you ask?" Pete asked.

"I just heard a rumor."

He gave her a sideways look.

"Yeah, a couple of amateurs went into Wild Boar Springs. Only one came out. I heard he got the bends—ascended like an idiot. Frankie actually got called to pull out the body." Pete jerked his head in the direction of his competition down the dock. His annoyance that the police called Frankie instead of him shone on his face like a neon sign. "God damn tourists think, 'oh, a cave, how cool, let's go see.' Fucking idiots."

"Pete, really? Watch your mouth in front of your daughter."

"Mom, it's not like I haven't heard it before," Kallie said. She was sitting in a dirty canvas chair amidst dusty gear in a corner. Now it was Andie's turn to roll her eyes. She looked from her daughter to her ex-husband.

"Whatever," she said. "Ok Pete, I'll see you at church on Sunday?"

Pete leaned across the scratched, yellowing plexiglass display cabinet and lowered his voice.

"Andie, can't I just bring her back tomorrow? I mean, I have students; I have to teach sometime."

Andie knew that Kallie could still hear him and her heart ached for her daughter.

"Don't be an asshole," Andie said in a half-whisper. Louder she said, "I'll see you Sunday." She walked to Kallie and kissed her on her head. She bent down and said into her ear, "If you need to come home earlier, call me; I'll come get you."

"Sure mom." Kallie's voice was dismissive, but Andie knew she was grateful for the offer.

As Andie walked towards the door, she said to Pete, "And don't pretend like I don't know about your 'students.' I still have the pictures."

As the bell over the door sounded, Andie heard Pete's voice call after her, "How many times I gotta tell you—that totally wasn't me!"

Chapter Four

When Andie got home, she grabbed a big glass of water and downed four ibuprofens. She gathered a book and headed into a hot bath. Athena plodded along happily next to her and settled onto the bathroom floor. Friends had told Andie the Jacuzzi tub was a waste of money, but at that moment, she couldn't imagine life without it.

The jets hit her back and feet. She draped a washcloth over her eyes and breathed in the steam, hoping to get rid of the dull headache that was threatening to engulf her entire skull. She tried to push her day out of her mind but could not stop thinking about her first patient. He certainly had the paperwork to prove he had the bends. His records from the hyperbaric medicine department at the local hospital definitely showed that he had ascended too quickly to the surface, and that nitrogen bubbles had formed in his blood.

Andie imagined how painful that must have been. On her honeymoon with Pete, she had experienced a mild case of the bends. She had a little dizziness and her fingertips and lips got numb, and that was after a rapid ascent from only forty feet. But Tony Siegel had cut through at least a hundred and fifty feet of water in a matter of seconds. He would have suffered a full-blown case of decompression sickness. She could almost feel the pain that he must have suffered in all of his joints. The pain, like a drill, would have moved into his muscles, and then deep into his bones, causing excruciating agony. The confusion, the numbness, the rash over his entire body... Andie had seen it before and did not wish that on anyone. Ultimately, the bends can be fatal if not treated quickly. It was lucky that he had access to a decompression chamber, and that he got there in time to prevent seizures, paralysis, and death.

Andie resituated the washcloth on her face in an attempt to settle her mind. She tried thinking about kayaking with Kallie, or her run in the morning. But she couldn't stop seeing his face in her mind's eye. His nose was healing from a recent fracture, one he said he sustained when he and his dive partner had become disoriented. He said his partner freaked out and thrashed around, that some flailing body part hit him in the face during the struggle, breaking his nose, and his dive mask.

But there was something about his eyes. The skin around his eyes had been swollen and was the sickly, chartreuse color of a receding bruise. Black eyes are common during a nose fracture, so that wasn't what bothered her, although it didn't help make him less disturbing. What Andie couldn't get over was the look in his eyes. He had been nervous, and she could tell he had tried hard to keep eye contact with her. This was the first thing that made her suspicious. Pete only looked her in the eyes if he was lying or if he wanted something from her.

The second thing was how blank his gaze had been. Andie had felt like the conversation happening in his head during the visit was so strong that he had to close off his mind completely in order to keep it from getting out. It was as if he wasn't careful, Andie would be able to hear his thoughts. Eleven years of medical practice had honed Andie's ability to read someone. She usually could tell when she was being lied to. She generally was very good at figuring out what the lie was, too, but this one had been difficult.

He had seemed so tormented. And his eyes…his eyes had just been so…dead.

***

When she woke the next morning, her headache was gone. She donned her running clothes and was happy to discover that the humidity had been replaced by fresh fall air.

She finished her run still full of energy. She showered and headed to the beach for her regular Saturday morning breakfast with her friends. When she arrived at The Cabana, she found two of her friends already seated on the deck. They had ordered her coffee and a plate of fruit. They all embraced and exchanged greetings.

"How's the baby, Maria?" Andie asked.

"Better, thanks. She was just getting a tooth."

Andie settled into her seat. She hung her bag on the back of her chair. "Where's Stacy?" She asked as she gazed contentedly out over the white sandy beach, to the azure blue waters of the Gulf of Mexico.

The smell of the ocean was stronger here than near her house, and it lacked any hint of decay, any suggestion that there was life other than the sea. The water was a blue-green that, try as they might, humans could never replicate. She knew that the water was warm, not because she had felt it recently, but because while the air temperature might vacillate at this time of year, the Gulf was always still warm in October. Most days it was as inviting as a warm bath—a tranquil, blue, salty bath.

She turned her eyes to the sky, which was a perfect shade of light blue. It was Andie's favorite color. It was also one of the reasons she chose The University of North Carolina for medical school; as far as she was concerned, Tar Heel blue was the best color in the world.

"She had a case she had to post early, but she said in her text she would be here," Maria answered. She gave Andie a look that said, 'except I know you don't check your messages unless it's your call service.'

Andie checked her phone and saw the group text she had missed.

"Oh, look at that—here it is," she said with a chuckle. "Aphrodite, how's work?" She took a sip of coffee and a bite of her fruit. The apples were bitter and the melon felt old and chewy. She pushed the plate away from her.

"Meh, fine. I had to throw a guy out last night—he got all handsy."

"Did Tank come in to help or did *you* actually have to deal with this guy yourself?" Andie asked. Aphrodite sat back and tossed her long black curls over her shoulder.

"You know what I mean, Tank threw the guy out."

Maria and Andie laughed.

"Occupational hazard, I guess," Maria said. "All I get is colds."

Aphrodite was a dancer. She was good, Broadway worthy actually. But she didn't fit in with the tall, skinny sticks in New York, so she had come home and now she worked freelance. Work for a short, curvy dancer was limited, however. Kallie and Andie took Aphrodite's belly dance class when time allowed, but sometimes teaching wasn't enough to pay the bills. That meant dancing at 'gentlemen's clubs' every now and then to supplement her income.

Andie saw Stacy step out of the main restaurant and head towards them. Stacy was tall, taller than Andie by far. She was Andie's opposite in most other ways as well. Where Andie had dark, curly hair, Stacy had ginger-blonde, straight hair. Andie's eyes were dark, her skin characteristically olive, giving away her Mediterranean heritage. Stacy was Greek as well, but her eyes and skin were fair. She always joked that her father must have been the mailman.

"Sorry I'm late, dead guy found in his house last night. The police insisted I post him this morning." Stacy was the Medical Examiner for the county north of them.

"Ooo, I read about that in the paper this morning," Maria said. "Home invasion or something like that...?"

"The dude was pumped full of narcs and benzos, so I'm sure if it was an invasion, he wouldn't have been able to fight anyone off," Stacy remarked dismissively. She picked up a piece of melon from Andie's discarded plate, but spit it back out almost immediately.

Everyone nodded. Drug-related deaths were way too common in this part of the state.

The waitress came by with coffee, and Stacy ordered breakfast.

"It's all those primary care docs handing out oxy like it's candy," Stacy said over the rim of her coffee mug. She winked at Andie. "Just kidding Andie. Sort of." She said the last couple of words under her breath.

"Don't hate on PCPs," Andie said. "You're the one who decided to hang out with the dead. I get wine and cookies at Christmas, you just get the remains of the victims of drunk driving."

"Eww, ladies, really?" Aphrodite exclaimed. "That was low, Andie."

Andie rubbed her eyes with the base of her palms.

"Sorry Stace," she said. "Speaking of dead bodies..."

Maria and Aphrodite sighed and sat back in their chairs.

"Every week, the doctor talk. You guys know this is annoying, right?" Maria said.

"No, no, I'm curious about that guy they dragged out of Wild Boar Springs last week. Did you guys hear about that?" Andie continued.

Aphrodite said no; Maria said she had. Stacy looked uncomfortable. "Stacy, did you get that post?" Andie asked.

"I did. I don't know if I'm supposed to talk about it though."

This caught Aphrodite's attention. "That sounds intriguing, do tell!" she said as she leaned forward.

"Didn't you hear her?" Maria said as she playfully tapped Aphrodite's arm. "She's not supposed to talk about it. But no, really, come on Stace, what happened?"

Andie tried to keep her face neutral. Stacy did not seem to be fooled, however. She looked at Andie through narrowed eyelids.

"Yeah, I haven't been told to not say anything, it's just... the investigation is still on-going," she said eventually.

"I thought it was a dive accident," said Maria. "The paper said that his partner got the bends, was taken down to Indian Rocks Hospital for decompression treatment. The story didn't say if he lived or not though."

Dive accidents, especially in any one of the caves and caverns that dotted the state, were also common. Usually an over confident open water SCUBA diver would go past the warning sign, telling people who are not trained to stay out of the cave. It's dark in the tunnels and people easily get disoriented. They run out of air and then someone has to go in and pull their body out.

"I hear he did," Andie said. She shifted in her seat as Stacy stared at her. "What?! I did! Pete told me."

Maria groaned. "God, Andie. Why do you even talk to him still?" she asked.

Andie sighed. "We've been over this, ok? For Kallie, it's for Kallie."

"How's that working out for you?" Stacy asked.

"He's still a pain in my ass." Andie's voice was muffled from where her face rested in her hands. "And Stacy, you should understand. You, too, Aphrodite—you know how the community gets! My poor mom has to answer questions about why we don't live together, and the kids at church look at Kallie... I just don't want her to get a reputation."

"For what?!" asked Maria. "For having divorced parents? Come on!"

"Look, the sins of the father and all of that. Divorce reflects poorly on the kids, at least in our community. It could even affect who she marries one day," Andie said defensively.

"That's so stupid," Stacy stated, shaking her head.

"Shut up, Stace. You don't have kids. Everyone just thinks you're a lesbian," Andie retorted.

"And I don't care! You should try it, Andie, try not caring what any of those old, judgmental *koutsomboles* think of you at church," Stacy said.

"I'm with Stacy," said Maria.

"Me too," added Aphrodite.

"Anyway!" Andie said. "Pete told me the guy with the bends lived."

"Please tell me he didn't tell you this when you gave in to a little post-divorce sex," Aphrodite asked.

"Oh, hell no," Andie answered. "We just chatted about it when I dropped Kallie off last night."

Another groan from Maria, this time she was joined by Aphrodite.

"So, he was actually there when you got there?" Aphrodite asked.

Pete had a habit of conveniently not being where he was supposed to be when it was time for the kid hand-off. He had all kinds of excuses, including 'I had to close and you were late.' Not that he couldn't text or call Andie to make other arrangements. That would be adult and responsible, two things Andie would never accuse Pete of being. Then he would conveniently not hear his phone all weekend. Andie didn't mind more time with Kallie, but it was the principle behind the behavior that made Andie want to strangle him.

"Oh, I made sure to make it before closing time," Andie answered.

Aphrodite mumbled something under her breath. Andie's friends were not Pete's biggest fans. Andie changed the subject back to the dive accident again.

"So Stacy, what was the post like for the dead diver?" she asked.

Stacy's light eyes lingered on Andie's face before she answered.

"My, you're persistent this morning, aren't you? The exam was not normal; it didn't show the normal drowning findings. I mean he definitely drowned, but there were other things. I had to call the police once I saw the bruising on his arms."

"This is getting better," Aphrodite said. "What kind of bruising?"

"Getting better, Aphrodite? A man died," Andie chuckled.

"You know what I mean," Aphrodite said. "It's getting more intriguing. Look, my life is full of drama because some men can't keep their hands to themselves. This is new and different drama for me."

"Fair enough," Andie replied.

"He had bruising on his cheek," Stacy continued, "and his lip was torn. It looked like his regulator had been forcefully removed from his mouth, like someone had ripped it out." She made a quick movement with her hand, mimicking tearing something away from her face. She continued, "The bruising on his arms was hard to find. He had been in the water for a few hours once they got him out, and by the time he got to me, he was decomposing already. But I definitely found hand-shaped bruises on his upper and lower arms."

Andie sat back and took a deep breath. This information did not surprise her. She knew that her gut feeling about Mr. Anthony Siegel had been strong. So strong in fact that it would not surprise her if he was capable of murder.

Chapter Five

The next morning Andie took a longer run than normal before church. She had worked at the jail in residency, so this was not her first time dealing with a patient who had committed murder. Still, however, it was unsettling. The cool fall air helped to clear her mind, which was good, because she felt like she was going to need all the strength she had to deal with her mother.

A few hours later, Andie met her mother, Sophia, on the steps of the ornate Greek Orthodox Church that she had been attending since she was a child. As Andie approached the imposing building, she saw her small mother standing on the immense white steps. Sophia was clad from head to toe in black, as she had been for the last thirty years since Andie's father had died. The black scarf she had tied around her head made her look like a morbid Russian nesting doll.

"*Andromeda mou!*" her mother embraced her as she scaled the marble stairs. Sophia linked her elbow through Andie's and they walked through the heavy wooden double doors of the church together.

Andie crossed herself with holy water as she entered the cool, dark cathedral. The vaulted ceilings always reminded her of the inside of an ornately carved boat, with arched bracers and whirls of wood. The walls of the church were covered in frescos, images of Saints, and of the Holy Family. Halos of gold encircled the heads of fair-haired cherubs, and the scent of incense permeated the hallowed space. Straight ahead, above the altar and under the gold and silvery images of angels, hung a lavish cross painted in shiny gold. A graphic depiction of Jesus hung woefully on the gilded wood.

When Andie was a child, she had asked her mother why the cross was so fancy.

"Wasn't Jesus killed as a punishment? Why would they give him such a pretty cross?" she had asked.

"Shhh," her mother admonished. "Jesus can hear every word you say."

Looking back on that now, Andie was sure her mother had prayed for her soul every night for a year just because of that question.

Andie and Sophia passed down the main aisle, greeting friends as they went. Many of the families they saw had been attending the church since before Andie was born. She had grown up with many of the children, watched them get married, lose loved ones. A few of them were also her patients. Andie was good at drawing boundaries, which was good, because in the Greek community in Tarpon Springs, everyone knew almost everyone else's business. She had to manage her doctor-patient relationships carefully. For example, when she knew that a husband was having an affair but was seeing the wife as a patient... it got complicated.

Together Andie and her mother chose a pew halfway to the front of the church. Andie sat near the aisle. She checked over her shoulder every few seconds, looking for Pete and Kallie.

"They will be here, *hara mou*," her mother said with a pat on her leg.

While she knew that was true, Andie held an irrational fear that one Sunday Pete would not bring Kallie back. She had thought up a million different scenarios as the years unfolded. Maybe he would take her on a chartered boat and not come back. Maybe he would run off with one of his 'students' and take Kallie with him. Whatever the story that haunted her head on any given day, the end result was the same: Andie never saw Kallie again.

She looked back up at the bloody Jesus. She had always wondered how a parent could have allowed that to happen to their child. She shook herself, trying to dispel her blasphemous thoughts. She concentrated on trying to calm her fears.

Growing up, Andie lived with the knowledge that she would always have a family. Not because she had aunts, cousins, brothers, or sisters around, because she didn't. She was an only child; she grew up watching her mother mourn her dead father. No, it was because her mother had told so many stories about Greece that Andie felt she had a country full of people just waiting to welcome her home.

But she also grew up knowing that her mother, perpetually dressed in black, perpetually mourning her dead husband, was not capable of supplying what she needed. Somewhere, somehow, Andie realized early in life that if she wanted something—a home, a car, food—she was going to have to stand squarely on her own two feet and make it happen.

This meant that every time someone in Greek school told her, 'You will find a Greek husband and make beautiful little Greek children,' Andie heard 'If you want to find a man who will be the center of your world, and breed like you are supposed to, you will have to find a way to follow your dreams in secret. You will have to create your own world of security, so that when said man and said children come along, you will be strong enough and capable enough to survive when he dies, and you are left with all of those beautiful Greek children, alone.' Frankly, just remembering those days was exhausting.

Finally, Andie saw the outline of her daughter and her ex-husband as they entered the church. She stood up and beckoned them towards where she and Sophia were sitting. As Kallie slid along the dark, polished wood seat, Andie hugged her tightly.

"Ow, mom," Kallie whispered. "I'm here, ok?"

The service started soon after they arrived. Nothing extraordinary happened during the mass. Andie did add a prayer for her patient, and for his possible victim. Otherwise, it was the same music, the same prayers, and the same sermon that Andie had heard for hundreds of Sundays throughout her life.

After the final prayer, they lined up to file out with the rest of the parishioners. Pete stepped into line next to Andie and put an arm around her shoulder. She ignored him.

"Oh, very nice," he crooned in her ear. "You like my arm? I know you like my arm, I know you like my..."

With a swift movement, Andie elbowed him hard in his abdomen. Pete doubled over, releasing a loud huff, and then an expletive. His voice echoed off of the ceiling and everyone around them stopped talking. Andie covered her mouth with her hand, just like the other women who were watching the scene. And just like the throng of other people who passed by the bent over man, Andie gazed around with a worried look on her face, trying to determine what in the world just happened. Pete looked up and glared at his ex-wife.

Eventually Andie bent over as though tending to him. She draped an arm over his back and leaned close to his face.

"You... are a slimy *malaka*. Don't ever touch me again," she said quietly. She fixed her face into a mask of worry and rubbed his back lovingly. She took his arm, pulled him upright, and led him down the aisle. Together they passed through the heavy front doors and out into the Florida sun.

***

"Remember, don't talk about Jordan, he's not Greek," Andie said to her daughter as they turned the corner on to the oak-lined street where Andie had grown up. Sunlight danced sporadically through the windshield. Spanish moss dripped off of ancient oak trees like living cobwebs. Andie slowed her old Volkswagen as she neared her childhood home.

"I know, Mom," Kallie said disdainfully.

"And when your grandmother talks about the car, just smile and nod."

"I know, Mom!"

"And don't let your father get to you," she said quietly.

"I'm going to pretend you kept that part to yourself," Kallie replied, "because I know you really meant, 'and I must remember not to let your father get to me.'"

"So wise, my little muse," Andie said. She reached over and tucked a strand of thick, black hair behind Kallie's ear. Kallie's smooth tresses were a far cry from Andie's unmanageable mess of curls. Kallie released a moody sigh reserved for mothers.

They pulled into the driveway of Sophia's pink, ranch-style blockhouse. Andie reflected that she needed to call the lawn company who maintained her mother's yard. The fountain that lived between the front walk and the garage was turning green in places.

Andie looked over at her fifteen-year-old child. "Shall we?" Andie continued. "It looks like your dad's not here yet." She looked over her shoulder at the road. There was no sign of Pete's Mercedes work van.

When Pete had opened the dive shop on the docks, he convinced Andie that he needed a van to cart around tanks and dive supplies. Andie agreed; she knew what it took to dive a cave in the middle of nowhere Florida. So, she had agreed to help him purchase a reliable vehicle so he could maintain his business.

What she did not agree to was using the loan she had co-signed, plus months of child support, to purchase a Mercedes.

"It's the safest thing out there," he had argued. "It will last forever!"

"It had better," Andie had responded before slamming the phone on the base, "because it is the last thing I help you buy."

Now she saw the van driving around town from time to time. When she did, she wished with her whole being that she had gone through the immense hassle of changing her last name when they got divorced. As it was, every time she saw the "Sun and Fun SCUBA" truck, she worried that her patients would think she had something to do with the images airbrushed on the side of the white vehicle.

"No one can dive The Parthenon, Pete, because it's not underwater," she had tried to tell him. "And Florida's not on the Mediterranean." The images of goddesses swimming in blue waters, of Zeus smiling down on SCUBA divers exploring Greek ruins, made Andie want to run and hide.

"Are we going in, or are you going to stare at the naked lady covered in algae for the rest of the day?" Kallie asked, bringing Andie back to what was in front of her.

Andie pulled her eyes away from the water that flowed out of the algae covered statue in the middle of the fountain. She shot a reproving look at her daughter.

"It's a good thing you're so cute or you wouldn't survive," she said as she opened the car door. The old springs creaked, and as the door went as far as it would go, there was a loud pop. Andie pushed the well-loved car door closed and a patch of rust fell from the undercarriage.

"We need a new car, mom. This thing is so embarrassing," Kallie said.

"Well there's always that thing," Andie pointed toward the garage, where she knew her mother's huge Lincoln Town Car was waiting for Kallie to turn sixteen.

Kallie rolled her eyes, "Ugggg, no way. I would rather die than be caught driving that monstrosity."

Andie looked towards the front door where her mother was waiting for them on the porch. Sophia shuffled the few feet to the cement stairs to meet them.

"*Kaliope mou!*" She crooned. She reached up and cupped Kallie's face in her gnarled hands. She pinched her granddaughter's cheeks and then pulled her down so she could plant a kiss on both sides.

"*Ti kanis* mama," Andie said when it was her turn to receive the wet kisses that always left a smear of orange lipstick behind.

"*Ime, kore mou. Y Petros*?" Sophia asked looking past them to the street. "He did not come with you? He was at church; did he have to work afterwards? No matter, he will be here. Come, come inside." She led them through the white, wrought-iron screen door. The metal seashell welded into the center of the bars was peeling and chipped. Andie made a mental note to get someone out to repaint it.

Once the door closed, Sophia latched the three different locks. She gazed up and down the street expectantly, and then turned back to Andie and Kallie.

"So big!" she said, pinching Kallie's cheeks again. "So beautiful, just like the Goddess, Aphrodite!" She trundled her way to the kitchen. Andie and Kallie moved past the plastic covered teal and pink living room set into the formal dining room.

The table was set like it always was on Sunday afternoons. There was a steaming plate of lamb in the center, surrounded by knots of Greek bread. A plate of fresh spanakopita, traditional Greek spinach pie, was piled high near the head of the table. An iridescent shell-shaped bowl held a robust salad covered in fresh feta and beets, and the moussaka was laid out artfully on an elaborate serving plate.

"*Cafe?*" Sophia held up a battered tin container that held thick, dark liquid.

"*Efharisto,* mama," Andie joined her mother in the kitchen and poured her own cup of the caffeinated sludge. Grounds fell to the bottom of the mug that was shaped like a Greek column. Andie took a jolting sip and felt comforted by the strong sweetness.

The front screen rattled. Pete's voice rang from the porch,

"*Ti kanis,* Sophia! *Kallie mou,* come let me in."

Kallie put down her journal where she had been writing poetry and skulked through the living room. Her feet made a high-pitched zipping sound as she dragged them along the plastic strip laid over the carpet.

She opened the locks but turned away from her father, where he stood with his arms open, waiting for a hug. She plopped back down in the ornate chair in the corner. The protective cover crinkled as she settled against the uncomfortable thick plastic.

Pete strode in to the kitchen and kissed Sophia on both cheeks. His facial hair had grown since church. It made him look like a balding vagabond. He had changed into work clothes, and the image of a half-naked woman hugging an anchor was splattered with old paint. Andie shook her head. If she had showed up in such clothes, she would get a stern lecture on disrespecting her family. But Pete was a man, so his actions were beyond rebuke.

Pete moved to Andie and dove forward towards her face, projecting himself squarely at her lips. She stiff-armed him, stopping his obnoxiously repetitive effort to obtain a kiss.

"Don't even think about it, *kerata*, you lost that right the minute you stuck your-" she said quietly. Her attempt to keep her words from her mother failed and Sophia cut her off.

"Andromeda! Do not speak to your husband that way!" Sophia reprimanded. "And when can I expect another grandchild?" she asked.

She linked her elbows through one of Andie's and then one of Pete's. She walked between them as they moved towards the dining room table. It was like having a dwarf dressed in black leading the way to the torture chamber.

Andie and Pete took their assigned seats next to each other. Pete smiled as he moved his chair closer to Andie. Andie looked sideways at him as she moved her chair further from him. She was ready with a fork when he reached under the table and put his hand on her leg.

"Oww! *Gamoto!*" he yelled. Sophia hit him hard on the back of his head.

"*Topedi*, your child is listening," she admonished him.

"Yaya, I'm fifteen, it's not like I haven't heard it before," Kallie called from the living room.

"Come eat, Kaliope," her grandmother responded. "You're too thin; you will not be able to bear sons with those small hips. Come, put some meat on your bones."

Kallie joined them at the table. Andie motioned for her to remove her headphones from her ears. Kallie begrudgingly complied.

"*Pater Imon...*," Sophia began. Together they finished the blessing. Then, as if choreographed, they all crossed themselves three times.

"So, when are you coming to get the car?" Sophia asked as she served moussaka to everyone.

"Soon," Andie responded. She stared at Kallie meaningfully. "We will see what we can do."

Andie's pocket vibrated. She retrieved her phone and saw that it was a page from her on-call service.

"No phones at the table, Andromeda," Sophia said. She tapped Andie's hand with a serving spoon covered in potato salad.

"It's work, Ma," Andie said. She wiped the mayonnaise off of her hand and pushed her chair back.

"So smart, my daughter," Andie heard her mother say to Pete and Kallie as she walked to the kitchen. "She's a doctor you know. I always knew things would be alright, eventually. What about you Kaliope, have you found a husband yet?"

"Yaya, I'm only fifteen," Kallie responded.

"I met your grandfather when I was only thirteen. We were married two years later…." Andie tuned out the familiar story about suffering in the Greek countryside, but how true love makes everything better. She started dialing the number to return the page as Sophia got to the part about how true love lasts forever, even after death.

"This is Dr. Markos, returning a page," Andie said as the emergency room doctor answered the phone, "…ok, thanks. Yeah, admit him to the hospitalist service. He has a history of reflux, so I'm sure he's been eating something he shouldn't, but still, he's ninety years old; it's always worth watching him for twenty-three hours… great, thanks."

"Mr. Papadopoulous?" her mother asked as Andie returned to the table.

"I'm not going to tell you, ma. Even if it were I wouldn't tell you," Andie replied.

Sophia tisked dismissively. "He was having chest pain after church, so I'm sure it is him. Andromeda, what will you do when I die? Will you even come and see me in the hospital if I get sick?"

"Ma, stop!" Andie put her face into her hands.

"What?" Sophia asked. "I'm an old lady, these things happen. I just want to see more grandchildren before I go, is that too much to ask?"

Pete put an arm around Andie's shoulders and squeezed. "I'm working on it, Sophia," he said with a wink in Andie's direction. Andie forcefully shrugged him off.

"Oh my god, I'm vomiting," Kallie exclaimed from across the table. She wretched dramatically into her moussaka.

"And I'm leaving," Andie said. She pushed back from the table, again. "Mama, I love you, but I can't do this. I am not having any more children with Pete, so love the one that I have. Come on Kallie, it's time to leave."

"See? You're too busy to even talk to your mother! Thirty years your father is gone, and I am all alone. I could die in my home and you would never know. Too busy being a doctor to notice. Go, *hara mou*, go live your life. I will be ok, I will clean up." Sophia stood up and started taking dishes to the kitchen.

"Mom!" Kallie whispered loudly through clenched teeth.

Andie put her hands on her hips and looked at the ceiling. She said a quick prayer, picked up the plate of lamb, and started helping her mother clear the table.

Chapter Six

It was the following Tuesday that Andie was paged in the middle of the night. Normally she kept her cell phone on vibrate, as she almost always had it somewhere near her body. When she slept, however, she turned the volume up as loud as it would go. It wasn't that she liked being woken up in the middle of the night, but she was a single practitioner, without any partners in her practice. This meant that she had to be available twenty-four hours a day, seven days a week, three hundred and sixty-five days a year. Constant call was exhausting mentally, and missing a call was a perpetual fear for Andie.

She chose the ring-tone she used for her on-call service carefully. It was a gentle sound, the soothing tinkling of bells that echoed off of the walls of an imagined Buddhist temple. It didn't matter how calm the sound was though, because after years of it signaling an incoming message from her call service, it still triggered a Pavlovian response. Andie's heart started to beat faster and a feeling of dread appeared in the pit of her stomach.

Andie heard the tinkling sound and her heart instantly began to race. She grudgingly rolled out of her warm spot under her comforter, over to the antique bedside table. The only light in the room filtered in from the street. She patted at the tabletop blindly, knocking a bottle of ibuprofen onto the ground. It hit the throw rug next to her bed with the sound of a child's plastic rattle.

Finally, she found her phone. She hit the screen blearily to stop the sound of the bells. When she saw the return phone number, she had a moment of relief, which was quickly replaced with another feeling of apprehension. It was the Tarpon Springs Police Department.

"This is Dr. Markos, I am returning a page," she said when a man's voice answered.

"Hey Andie, it's Sean."

Sean was a friend from high school. When they were teenagers, Sean had been a really nice guy. Everyone thought he would grow up to work in the hospitality industry in some way—a a concierge, maybe managing a big hotel on the beach. He surprised all of their friends by becoming a police officer for the City of Tarpon Springs, like his father.

"Hey Sean, what's up? And by what's up I mean why are you paging me at eleven at night? Because while I would love to catch up, it's eleven at night and you woke me up."

"Eleven PM is the middle of my work day, so I know you might be cranky because I woke you up, but I'm just trying to get my job done."

Andie sat up in bed and rubbed her eyes. She turned on the bedside light and grabbed the pen and paper she kept there for just this reason. Years in internship and residency had made Andie very effective if she had to jump out of bed for a life-threatening situation. However, as the years went by, and the adrenaline associated with the potential for an immediate emergency waned, she needed to write things down when she got paged in the middle of the night.

"Sorry Sean, of course. Let me start again: Officer Malone, good evening, what can I do for you, and the Tarpon Springs Police Department, as the Doctor on call for Markos Family Medicine?"

"Not much better, the sarcasm is a little much, just saying."

"What the hell do you want?" Andie finally said. "Did someone break into my office, die, or forge a prescription? Cuz those are the reasons the cops page me in the middle of the night. Otherwise, I'm sure it can wait until morning."

"One of your patients is dead," he said.

Oh shit, Andie thought. She sighed.

Her voice softened, "Ok, really, I'm sorry; I didn't mean to be insensitive. You know me; my mouth gets me in trouble all of the time. Who is it?"

"Anthony Siegel," Sean said. "We found your name and an order for a..." He started to read something "...Contrast enhanced Computed Tomog-"

Andie interrupted him, "A CT scan, yeah. I wrote that when I saw him."

"Looks like he won't need that now."

"*Now* who's being insensitive?"

She pinched the bridge of her nose between her thumb and her forefinger, and closed her eyes.

"The guy was a murder suspect, ok?" Sean said. "We were coming to take him in, so cut me some slack. You're the one who has that hypocritical oath."

"Hippocratic."

"Whatever. Anyway, since Stacy did the original post on his alleged victim, the ME for Pinellas said it was ok to call her in. Thought you'd want to know." Even though he said it was the middle of his shift, Sean sounded tired. No matter how much sleep you get, the night shift is rough.

"So, you're calling me just to inform me of his passing? Because I know there won't be a death certificate for me to sign."

"I'm calling you because I need all of the notes you have on him," Sean said.

"Jesus, Sean, that couldn't wait until morning?" Andie was wide awake now.

She heard Sean chuckle. "No, it couldn't." He paused, "Ok, I've had my fun. Yes, I need your notes, but the real reason I'm paging you is because Stacy asked me to call you. She wants you to meet her at the victim's house."

"Really, you couldn't have led with that?" Andie was up and trying to dress while not dropping the phone. "Why didn't Stacy call me herself?"

"I thought it would be more fun this way," Sean said.

"I dislike you now more than before," she said as she hit the end button on her phone.

Ok, maybe they had been more than friends in high school.

***

Andie drove towards route 19, the six-lane highway that ran north and south through Pinellas County. Developers had taken over in recent years and the part of the road that ran past the edge of Tarpon Springs was like strip mall hell. Andie made the best of it though, counting on a Starbucks every couple of blocks. She pulled through a twenty-four hour drive through and grabbed an espresso on her way to the scene.

Her GPS dumped her into an older neighborhood, full of poorly maintained homes and broken-down cars. Many lawns were overgrown, and more than one building had a sign on the door declaring it condemned. Andie followed the last few directions given by the computerized voice. When she had the thing installed in her old Volkswagen, the pimple-faced kid asked her what vocal sound she wanted. Andie was unaware she had a choice, but in the end she chose an Australian male. It somehow felt better taking directions from a sexy Australian man.

She turned the last corner and did not have to guess which house was her destination. Blue and red lights strobed quietly against the weeds and decaying cinder block structures. Andie parked a block away. When she reached the police tape at the front of the house the officer had to call Sean to get permission to let her pass.

"He says you can go on in. They are in the back. He says, um, don't touch anything on the way through," the young uniformed man relayed.

Andie pinched his cheeks. "Thanks Nick. And tell your mom I say hello."

He smiled and a dimple popped out to the left of his lips, "Will do, Dr. Markos."

The air inside the house was uncomfortably warm. The scent of death hung heavily in the air. It mixed with the odor of old cigarettes and bad Chinese take-out, and the resultant smell made Andie cover her nose with the sleeve of her sweatshirt. As she walked through the dirty living room, she saw the scattered debris of a bachelor's home. She heard the flies buzzing around old Kung Pow chicken as she moved into the bedroom.

"*Ti kanis,* mama," Stacy said. She kissed Andie on the cheeks.

"Did you really have Sean call me and wake me up?" Andie asked.

Stacy threw her head back and laughed. "He said he wanted to, and I didn't want to ruin his fun. Come on, don't you miss being called to see a patient in the middle of the night?"

Andie looked at her with one eyebrow raised. "No. I do not miss it at all."

"Miss what?" a male voice asked behind her.

Andie spun around and saw Detective Sean Malone standing in the doorway from the kitchen. His dark auburn hair was tousled; his dress shirt was clean and carefully tucked in to khaki pants. Andie noted his matching belt and shoes, and Sean noted Andie looking him up and down.

"What?" He asked, looking down at himself. "Did I get blood on me?" He inspected his pants and the arms of his button-down shirt.

"Not that I can see, but the night is young." Andie turned back around and faced the bed. She took in the horrifying scene of her dead patient.

There wasn't blood everywhere. Nor was he dismembered and strewn around the room. The scene was disturbing due to the unnatural positioning the dead man had assumed in the last painful moments of his life.

The body was contorted. His hands were frozen, spread and grasping, like petrified claws. His back was bowed like he had reared up, ready to strike, but had died before he could reach his prey. The most disconcerting site was his face. Like a macabre death mask seen in a museum, his mouth was pulled down at the sides, a permanent grimace of anger, fear, and pain. All of the muscles and tendons in his neck were contracted and taut. His toes were spread and permanently flexed. They pointed at the ceiling like one last cry for help.

Both Andie and Stacy stared at the twisted corpse in front of them. The officers in the room were still, waiting for direction. But neither of the women gave any. Finally, Stacy spoke.

"Andie, oh my god. Do you know what this looks like?" she asked.

"Almost exactly like it," Andie replied.

"I won't know until I get him on the table, but I would put money on it," Stacy added.

Sean sighed and slowly ran his hands through his hair.

"Ladies, sorry, *Doctors*... whatever IT may be, can we get this guy outta here so we can start our search?" he said. The women turned around simultaneously. Stacy's eyebrows shot up; Andie laughed.

"Do your thing, Detective," Andie said. She patted Sean on the arm as she passed by on her way out of the room.

As she moved back through the debris in the living room she heard Stacy's official voice behind her, "Do your best to get him in the bag, but you may have to get the extra-large sack from the van."

Andie walked out on to the front porch of the rundown bungalow. The night was cool but the humidity had returned. The saturated air hugged her skin. Andie drew in a deep breath, trying to purge the stench of decay and moldy fried rice from her nose.

She moved slowly down the rotting stairs. Assistants from the medical examiner's office walked past her with a gurney and a large black, plastic bag. In the few seconds it took for them to pass, Andie caught a whiff of formaldehyde, plastic, and death. She flashed back to anatomy lab. She took in another deep breath, drawing in a lungful of humid Florida air through her nose. She was still trying to clear her nostrils from this most recent brush with the characteristic smell of a dead body. It didn't work. Andie felt like the scent would be with her forever.

She knew it was none of her business; she knew that she needed to keep her nose out of this. No matter how she tried, however, she could not get the image of her twisted patient out of her mind. A page in the middle of the night and a suspicious patient dead from a rarely seen disease; it was too much, too intriguing. Andie was drawn in.

Chapter Seven

Stacy followed the body out of the house. She joined Andie in the driveway. Tall weeds grew freely amidst the small, bleached shells that must have been attractive once upon a time. Now the native flora seemed to be returning the area to its natural state.

"Where in the hell did he get tetanus?" Andie asked.

Stacy shook her head. "Diving maybe? I'll tell you what though, I know how he got it. There was a large gash on his arm; it looked about three days old."

Andie shook her head. "He wouldn't have gone diving again, not after his decompression sickness, and he didn't have that wound when I saw him. Trauma doesn't surprise me though. If he did kill that diver, the one we talked about on Saturday, then I'm sure he didn't get stabbed by hanging out with his grandmother at church."

Stacy gave her a look that clearly said, 'I knew you were hiding something,' but she didn't say anything else; she moved on.

"Church can get hairy," she said. "I've sat behind you and Pete during services. I wouldn't have been surprised if you whipped out a knife during The Peace and buried it between his shoulder blades."

Andie gave a sardonic snort.

"Did you ever think about it, Andie? Seriously." Stacy turned to face her. "All of those women...you must have been tempted. I mean a little pressure in the right place on his neck, a well-placed syringe... No one would ever know."

"God, Stacy, really?"

Stacy threw her hands in the air in a gesture of surrender.

"You need to get out of that morgue," added Andie.

One of the young men in dark blue windbreakers approached from the coroner's van. The shells crunched in the sickly yellow light of the old streetlamp.

"Dr. Antonitis, we have him in the van. Are you meeting us back at the office, or are you waiting until tomorrow to do the post?" he asked.

The stairs groaned behind them and Andie turned to see Sean coming towards them.

"What's this?" Sean asked.

"I was just telling my intern that I will be doing the post in the morning," Stacy responded.

Sean put his hands out to his side, palms up.

"Come on, Doc! You have to give me something."

"Ok," Stacy relented, "and do not quote me on this, but he likely died of tetanus, which was likely introduced via the laceration on his arm. But if you put that anywhere official I will deny that I ever said it."

"Tetanus? Don't we get a vaccine for that?" Sean asked.

"Sadly, not always," Andie chimed in. "There has been a huge anti-vaccine movement in the US recently. I hate to say it, but I kinda hope this *is* tetanus. Maybe that'll show those fanatics why we developed the vaccine in the first place."

"All I know is that this guy," Stacy jabbed her thumb over her shoulder, "had a full-blown case that progressed really quickly. Also, the wound on his arm looked like a defensive wound, not an accidental slash. While the cut did not kill him directly, this is manslaughter at the least, and just maybe a homicide."

***

After work the next day, Andie drove up to the Medical Examiner's office to see the body and talk to Stacy. She waited behind the glass partition that separated the autopsy suite from the viewing room. The curtain was drawn to the side and Andie had a full view of all of the metal tables, and of Stacy hard at work. Stacy was dressed in full protective gear, complete with a facemask and shoe covers. The shrill sound of the bone saw carried through the glass. Andie watched as she cut through the skull of the pale body on the table closest to the door.

She took a seat in one of the black, government issued, molded plastic chairs. The room she was in was dark, sterile. It smelled like the rest of the building—death, formaldehyde, and cleaning fluid. The room felt old and forgotten. The back wall was painted brown and the side walls were a sickly shade of beige. The floor was institutional green tile. It felt like no one paid attention to this room, like no one bothered to update the space where some people experienced the worst moment of their lives.

The only window was the one that looked out towards the dead bodies. There was a door on each of the beige walls. One would take a visitor deeper into the office, deeper towards paperwork and their loved ones remains. The other led to the exit.

Andie watched as Stacy removed organs, weighed them, and filled out paperwork. She checked her watch a few times and texted Kallie that she was going to be home late, but she left out information about why. Teenager drama would only flourish with the information that Andie was at the morgue.

Eventually, Stacy expertly threaded thick, durable, black medical string through the eye of a large needle. It reminded Andie of the darning needle her mother used to piece together the countless afghans she made. Quickly, Stacy sewed up the gaping Y in the dead man's chest. When it looked like she was done, Andie tapped on the window. Stacy jerked her head towards the exit, and Andie left the small depressing room through the egress leading deeper into the cold building. She met Stacy outside of the heavy industrial door that led out of the autopsy suite.

"Definitely Tetanus," Stacy said. The scent of the dissection wafted on a puff of air as the pneumatic hinge eased the thick door closed. "Cause of death was cardiopulmonary failure secondary to tetany of the diaphragm. The wound was gnarly, too. I took tissue samples and gave them to Sean."

"Sean was here?"

"Earlier this morning—he came to see the autopsy." She eyed Andie and smiled. "It was good to see him last night, right? He's looking good, don't you think?" She winked.

Andie rolled her eyes and crossed her arms.

"Is that why you had him call me? Is this your not-so-subtle way of trying to find me a man?"

"Maybe..." Stacy continued. She took off her booties and paper gown and threw them through the slotted top of a nearby cardboard drum.

"I need a man like I need a hole in my head," Andie said.

"Oh, my dear," Stacy put a hand on Andie's shoulder. "What you need is a real man, because that slime ball piece of shit that fathered your amazing daughter does not qualify. I don't think you know what you're missing."

Andie looked at her watch again. "What I'm missing is dinner with said amazing, albeit moody, daughter, so if there's nothing else for me to know about the autopsy, I'll talk to you later." She moved to kiss Stacy on the cheeks. As she got closer, however, she thought better of it; the smell of the autopsy was still strong. Her face bunched up and she pulled away. "Oh Stace, I don't know how you do it."

"Just think about it," Stacy said gently.

"About leaving Family Medicine and joining the death squad? No thanks, I'm good; I'll keep my private practice." Andie walked towards the exit.

"No, and don't be stubborn. About Sean; think about Sean."

Andie turned when she reached the door and looked back at her best friend.

"I'll talk to you later, Stacy." She smiled and left.

***

Friday came quickly.

"God damn you, Pete!" Andie exclaimed as she peered through the dirty glass of *Sun and Fun SCUBA*. The store was dark and empty. "It's not even six," she said under her breath. She looked at her watch and then looked around the marina, like he might magically appear nearby.

"It's ok, mom, I really don't want to go anyway," Kallie said. She was leaning against the worn wood that made up the outside of the old building.

Andie sighed. "Come on, honey, let's watch the sun set."

She linked her arm through Kallie's bent elbow and urged her towards the end of the Sponge Docks. There was an area with benches that extended into the intercoastal waterway. Andie had fond memories of sitting with her mother on the benches, watching the boats come in and out of the harbor.

Together, Andie and Kallie strolled down the dock. Andie only looked over her shoulder once to see if Pete had shown up. They had not gone far when Andie saw that the next light on, the next store that appeared to still be open at that time of night, was outside of Pete's biggest competitor, *Fin Fun Charters*. Two people stepped out of the shop. They were silhouetted against the evening sun, which now low in the sky. Andie shielded her eyes t better.

It was clear that they were engaged in a heated argument. One man was larger and rounder than the other, and Andie assumed this was the owner of *Fin Fun Charters,* Frankie. She had known Frankie since she left for medical school. They were never close; Andie always felt that he cared more about profit than doing what was right. He also seemed to take unnecessary risks when he dove. As a diver, she felt that there were some things that should not be done, not for any amount of money. Still, he had always been friendly to her.

Suddenly Frankie lunged at the smaller man. With surprising strength, the skinny one pushed Frankie away from him. Frankie stumbled, falling against the clapboard side of his storefront. He quickly recovered, and in a few steps, he reached out and shoved the skinny man towards the rail of the dock. The smaller man rushed at him and Frankie pulled back his arm. With a solid blow to the face, the skinny man stumbled backwards and went over the railing, into the dirty water of the harbor.

Chapter Eight

Andie dropped her bag and ran towards where Frankie was staring dumbly down at his victim, who was now floating face down in the small, choppy waves. As she vaulted over the rail, she looked quickly at his face. Frankie looked legitimately surprised at what was happening, as if he didn't believe he could hit someone hard enough to send them flying over a dock railing.

Andie hit the water feet first. She had lost her flip-flops on the run down the old dock, so as her feet hit the bottom, they impacted hard against the muscle shells that invariably clung to pilings and rocky shallows throughout the region. She felt the razor-sharp shells slice through her skin and she cursed. She looked down and saw the water around her feet darken.

She focused her attention back to the limp outline of the skinny man. She pulled herself towards him. He was small, but the weight of his wet clothes had dragged him under the surface and he was now floating close to the anchor of a nearby boat. Andie's eyes burned as gas-tinged saltwater assaulted her membranes. She reached the body and wrapped an arm around his waist. She had to move towards the anchor line so she could push off. She gritted her teeth as the pain from the cuts on her feet shot up through her legs and into her back.

God dammit, she thought to herself as she rocketed towards the surface. Andie hated the inconvenience of illness or injury. If it was not immediately going to kill her, she would rather pretend that it was not happening, and continue to go along with life as usual.

A small crowd had gathered in the dying light of the sunset. Kallie was bent over the rail and as Andie's head broke the surface, she heard her daughter scream, "Mom!"

"Call...911," Andie yelled, trying to catch her breath.

She turned over the motionless body she was holding. He wasn't breathing, but she found a pulse on his neck. She started giving mouth-to-mouth resuscitation, but the mix of trying to hold him up and tread water at the same time meant the amount of air that went in wasn't as large as it needed to be. She yelled to the people on the dock.

"Someone! Can... I... get some help?"

Frankie stood there lamely, expressionless. A tourist standing nearby handed the child he had on his hip to his wife and jumped in to help. Andie started swimming towards a ladder and the man met her half way there.

"He's not breathing, but he's got a pulse," she said. For the first time, she noticed blood coming from the unconscious man's nose and she cursed again. "Quick, we have to get out," she said to the second rescuer.

The ambulance arrived as they hoisted the limp body to the top of the access ladder. The whole dock shook as the medics ran towards them. Andie gave a quick run-down on what had happened, complete with weak pulse in the carotid and no breathing. Two of the uniformed men cut off the unresponsive man's shirt and started resuscitation efforts.

An older medic who appeared to be in charge held a metal clipboard box. He knelt next to Andie and was taking notes as she spoke.

"Oh, it sounds like you've had some training, that's great," he said. "Are you a nurse or did you take a CPR class at the YMCA?"

Andie stared at him blankly. She blinked, leaving her lids down for a long moment. She did not have the energy to have this conversation; she was too tired to have to explain that, just because she was a woman, does not mean that she is a nurse. Not that there was anything wrong with being a nurse, it just got tiring correcting people on a regular basis.

"Something like that," she finally said. She crawled to a nearby bench and watched as the skinny man she had rescued started to sputter. The medics rolled him on his side and water spilled from his mouth.

Andie turned and looked for Frankie. The crowd was larger now; she was sure that the lights and sounds of the ambulance had pulled people out onto the docks from the street. Even as she stood up on the bench, however, even as her feet left bloody footprints as she rose up onto her tiptoes, Frankie was nowhere to be seen.

***

"Andie, what the hell happened?" Sean grabbed her by the shoulders and spun her to face him.

"Easy!" she yelled. The pain of the sudden movement caused her to catch her breath. The medic who was taking care of her came up and placed a blanket around her shoulders. He led her back to the bench and started taking her vitals.

"I'm fine," she said to the handsome young man. She waved him off like she might a mosquito.

Kallie sat down next to her and looked worried.

"Don't listen to her, keep going," Sean interjected. Andie glared at him as a thermometer probe was stuck under her tongue. Eventually the little machine beeped.

"97.8," the medic said. "You're too cold. You should change clothes as soon as you can."

Andie waved him off again. Neither man moved.

"Fine!" she said.

Kallie told the medic about Andie's feet. Her eyes lingered on his tight uniform where the blue shirt hugged his upper arms.

"You're fine, huh?" Sean said. "I hear you can get, like, rabies from clams and stuff." He smiled.

"Stick to police work, Sean," retorted Andie.

The medic began to clean the wounds. Andie managed to not kick him in the face, which she took as a win.

"You should let us take you to the hospital, ma'am," the young man said. "We need to get you warmed up, and we can close the lacerations on your feet more efficiently in the ER."

"Not a chance," Andie said. "Do you have any mupirocin in that little box? Just put some of that on with a pressure bandage and we should be good."

"You'll have to sign the refusal form," the buff medic said.

"Yeah, yeah, sure thing." Andie saw Kallie's eyes lingering on the young man's arms as he gathered what he needed out of his gear box.

"What's your name?" Andie asked.

"Damian," the medic said with a smile.

"I'm Andie. This is my daughter, Kaliope."

"Kaliope, isn't that one of the muses?" Damian asked.

Andie looked at Kallie, prompting her to answer for herself. Kallie smiled and nodded.

"Yes, she was the muse of poets," Kallie said.

"With an angelic voice," Damian said, "If I'm remembering my mythology correctly."

Kallie smiled and looked at the ground. Damian's hands fumbled with the gauze he was holding.

"She's fifteen, by the way, so flirting is as far as this is going right now. And are you going to put that kerlex on, or do you want to just give it to me and I'll stop my own bleeding?" Andie interrupted their awkward moment. Kallie turned bright red and clicked her tongue at her mother in anger. She crossed her arms and turned away.

Damian finished cleaning Andie's feet. He put antibacterial ointment on the wounds and then wrapped them tightly. He handed her the left-over roll of fluffy white gauze and told her to keep the wound clean and dry, and to change the bandages once a day until she could see her doctor.

"She'll be sixteen in four months," Andie whispered to him. "How old are you?"

"Um, nineteen," Damian said uncomfortably. He tried three times to lock his gearbox before he was successful.

"Are you Greek?" Andie asked.

"Mom!" Kallie cried. Andie ignored her.

"My mother's Greek," Damian answered as he stood up. "And I will get you the form to sign." He turned to Kallie and flashed an awkward smile; he quickly walked away.

"God, mom! Could you have been more embarrassing?!"

"I'm sure I could've been. Would you like me to call him back over and give it another try? Come on Kallie, he was totally cute! I saw you looking at those nice, tan muscles. But just so you know, you're not allowed to go out with him until you're eighteen, and until he meets your grandmother and your father. Scratch that, we'll just bring him to meet Yaya."

A sound of aggravated embarrassment escaped Kallie's mouth.

Andie signed the refusal form and gathered her belongings, ready to leave the dock. Her feet were sore when she stood up on the rough wood, but she felt like she could make it to the car. Sean put an arm around her waist to support her, but she pulled away. The gauze on her feet was bulky and cumbersome. Her knees buckled in response to the pain as she belligerently refused his assistance.

"I'm fine, I can do it myself," she said through gritted teeth. She took a few hobbling steps towards her car.

"Come on, I'll take you home," Sean said.

"No, I have my car," Andie said. "Kallie can take me home."

Sean gave her a dubious look.

"I have my permit!" Kallie exclaimed.

"But you know what," Andie added. She was starting to shiver. "If you want, you can follow us. I know you have questions you have to ask."

Sean ran his fingers through his dark russet hair and looked around.

"Sure, fine, yeah. Let me tie this scene up and then I'll be there."

"You offered to give me a ride home, Sean. Were you just going to let me freeze here while you 'tied the scene up'? Come on Kallie, let's go." Andie put an arm around her daughter, who pulled away from Andie with a comment about her wet clothes. Together they shuffled back to the street.

"No, I mean, Andie!" Sean called after them. He threw his arms out to his side and sighed before turning back to talk to his officers.

Chapter Nine

Andie was out of the shower and in sweats when Sean arrived. Athena barked at the knock on the door, and when Kallie let him in, Athena stood solid, blocking the entire front hall. She smelled as much of Sean as she could reach, and after a last sniff at his backside she huffed a final breath and trotted back to Andie. She settled into the couch, taking up two of the three large cushions.

Andie was wrapped in a blanket in the only space left on the leather sofa, sipping hot tea. Her feet were propped up on an ottoman. A small amount of blood was coming through the bottom of the gauze. She shook her head at Sean when he came in to the living room.

"What?!" he exclaimed. He looked around and then chose a leather armchair in the corner.

"It's just that some things never change," Andie said. She smiled in spite of herself. "Over committing yourself is a hard habit to break."

Sean shrugged and chuckled.

"Did you ever think that maybe it's just you?"

It was Andie's turn to laugh.

"You mean it's my fault that you say yes to everything, and everyone, when you don't even know if you can fulfill your commitment?"

He considered her through familiar deep blue eyes.

"Yeah, that's what I'm saying."

Andie felt uncomfortable as he gazed at her without blinking. She looked down into her steaming drink. After a moment of silence, Sean spoke again.

"Can you tell me what happened?" He had his flip pad out and was poised to take notes.

Andie relayed her memory of the event. "I looked for Frankie in the crowd when I got out of the water, but he was gone."

"Did you hear any words between the two men?" Sean asked.

Andie's phone buzzed next to her. She picked it up and read the text.

"Stacy is asking for the third time if I need anything. Did you call her?"

"Maybe," he responded.

"Oh my god, what is wrong with men? Can you not trust a woman to take care of herself?"

"Can you perhaps let someone help to take care of you once in a while?"

She glared at him.

"No. No, I can't," she said.

"Typical."

Their tiff was interrupted by Kallie's appearance in the archway between the living and dining rooms.

"Mom, I'm going out with Jordan," she said.

"Let's try this again: Mom, can I go out with Jordan?" Andie retorted. Kallie groaned and rolled her head around dramatically.

"Yeah, that. Can I?" she asked. She didn't wait for an answer; she turned and walked back into the dining room.

"Oh, my god," Andie said to Sean. "The teenage years are totally going to kill me. Like, I really think I am going to spontaneously implode from the snark and attitude."

"Yeah, since it's all about you," Kallie said from the dining room.

"I'm sorry, *Kallie mou*, I forgot, it *is* actually all about you," Andie responded.

"What did you say about snark and attitude?" Sean asked.

"Really?" Andie said to him. "Stay out of this."

"I'm just saying, that apple didn't fall too far from the tree," he responded.

Kallie came back into the room wearing a jacket and carrying a bag.

"Jordan's outside waiting," she said.

Andie sighed.

"Ok baby, but let me tell you how this is going to go next time, or you won't be going anywhere. Stay with me here: 'Mom, Jordan called and wants to know if I can go out with him, is that ok? He's actually waiting outside, would you like him to come in before I go?' 'Why yes, my love, thank you, I would love to chat with him before you take off into a dark, Friday night with him. And thank you for being so forthright with your information and for asking for permission.' Got it?"

"Oh emm gee, Mom, you are so annoying."

"Oh emm gee, my sweet baby, I love you."

Kallie came and kissed Andie on the top of her head.

"I love you too," she said. She pointed a finger at Andie, and then at Sean. "Speaking of Friday night, don't get crazy now you two."

Sean held his hands up.

"Don't encourage her, Sean. And Kallie—just be home by eleven," Andie said.

"Sure thing, Mom," Kallie said over her shoulder as she closed the front door behind her.

***

The next morning was cold. Andie was the first one to arrive at The Cabana for Saturday breakfast. She chose a table inside. It was the first time since mid-summer that the friends didn't dine on the deck, when it had been so hellishly hot that they needed to be in the air conditioning. Aphrodite came in with a hat and scarf on. Maria followed in a down coat. Stacy was equally as bundled in jogging pants and a hooded sweatshirt. She had the hood up, with the string drawn around her face.

"It's freezing!" Aphrodite said as she settled into her seat.

"It's fifty-nine degrees," Andie laughed. Medical school in North Carolina had given her some perspective on 'cold.' Not much, but some.

"Right?! Like what the hell is that about?" Aphrodite replied.

"Andie, what happened last night?" Maria asked. "Stacy called and told me you went into the marina after some guy?"

"The story was in the paper this morning, too," Aphrodite said. "There was a piece about you, but it said that they didn't know who the guy was; that he refused care from the ambulance and then he disappeared from the scene."

"You read the paper?" Stacy asked.

Aphrodite glared at her. She shifted and then responded, "There was a review of my show. I saw Andie's name as I leafed through on my way to the Entertainment section." She lowered her eyes and took a sip of coffee.

Aphrodite prided herself on being ignorant of current events. She said that the news depressed her.

Andie reached over and gave Aphrodite's arm a squeeze. "I saw your review," she said. "It looked great."

"Thank you, honey," Aphrodite smiled.

"So, back to Andie," Maria said pointedly. "You saved a guy and you don't even know who he is? How interesting…"

Andie told her friends the story.

"What did Sean say?" Stacy asked.

"That he got a call about the disturbance while he was on his way to the docks to investigate something having to do with the diving death. All I know is that one of my patients, and the guy who died in the cave, are both related somehow to another investigation he has going on," answered Andie.

"Does he think the guy you rescued is involved in both things?" Aphrodite asked.

Andie shook her head, "I don't know, he didn't say. But since we don't know who the guy I fished out is, it's going to be hard to say what he's involved in." She took a sip of coffee. "Would I totally go to hell if I say that I hope Pete is involved, too?" They all laughed.

"Not at all, mama," Maria said. "Does Sean think that Pete is involved?"

"He didn't say," Andie replied.

"Well, what did he say?" Aphrodite asked. "And I'm not just talking about the case, if you know what I mean." She raised her eyebrows and smiled like the Cheshire Cat. "I mean, if you don't want to get too graphic, I totally get it... wait, no I don't. Tell us all the dirty details."

Andie gave her a glare she usually reserved for Kallie. She ignored her friend's comments.

"All I know is that there's something funny going on at the docks," Andie responded.

"Seriously, Andie?" Stacy laughed.

"What?!"

Stacy affected a Daffy Duck accent, "'Therth thomthing funny going on at the docths.'"

Andie glared at her but laughed in spite of herself.

"Obviously there's something going on down there," Aphrodite said.

"I'm actually meeting Sean at the docks after breakfast," Stacy said.

"Me too," Andie said.

"Interesting... Can he not do his job without you?" Maria asked.

Again, Andie scowled at one of her friends. "He told me he wanted me to make introductions."

"Is that what we're calling it these days?" Maria asked with a smile.

Andie ignored her. "Do you know why he asked you to come too, Stace?"

Stacy shrugged. "I don't know; to make sure you don't go in the water again?"

"Yeah, that must be it," Andie retorted dryly.

Chapter Ten

After breakfast, Stacy and Andie drove together in Stacy's sports car, her midlife crisis, to meet Sean at the docks. They left Andie's Volkswagen at the beach; Stacy would take her back to get it later. Andie's feet were sore from the night before, so the less she had to do the better.

Sean was waiting for them near the street, next to a bronze statue of a sponge diver. The antique diving helmet that topped off the statue gave the piece of art an otherworldly quality.

"Andie, are you ok walking?" he asked.

Andie could see concern in his eyes. She smiled.

"I might just have to go slow."

"You want me to go rent you a scooter?" Stacy asked. "Cuz I know this place just down the block, you know, they've got Hover Rounds and everything." She jerked her thumb over her shoulder towards downtown.

Andie had worn the only shoes that would fit over the guaze—a pair of athletic slides she used after running. Her feet still throbbed, but she was too stubborn to let someone push her around in a wheelchair.

"No, but when I need one I will come to you to sign the paperwork for my insurance, ok?" she retorted.

Together, the three of them moved towards the row of shops that lined the Sponge Docks in downtown Tarpon Springs. They stopped first at Pete's store, but the 'Closed' sign was visible in the door. The peeling window detail clearly read that store hours on Saturday were from 11-6. Andie checked her watch. It was 11:45 but the windows were dark and the door was locked.

"Maybe Pete did have something to do with this after all," Stacy said.

"You think Pete is involved in this?" Sean asked. Andie had her hands cupped against the dark glass. She was squinting into the cluttered store to see if she could glean any information.

"Nah, I was just hoping," she said. She pulled away and faced the other two. "What is 'this' anyway, huh Sean?"

He took in a deep breath, as if stealing time to think up a response. Stacy snatched a handful of folded paper from Sean's back pocket.

"Stacy, that's police information," he protested.

"Hey," she said, "I'm an officer of the court, so no worries."

Stacy was much taller than Andie, so she brought the paper down to where Andie could see what was printed.

"These are search warrants," Andie said. "For Pete's shop...for all of the fishing and dive shops along here. Sean, come on, what's going on?"

Sean sighed again. This time it was a sound of defeat.

"Ok, fine. Do you remember that missing person's case from a month ago?"

"The diver from up north?" Andie asked.

Stacy piped up, "Yeah, he came down for a dive trip but never made it home, right?"

"Right," responded Sean. "Cops found evidence of the trip in his apartment in Pennsylvania. There were emails he exchanged with three guys here in Florida. It looks like they planned a dive trip somewhere in the state. We couldn't find out where exactly, but it was obvious they were preparing to go underground. We found receipts for camping gear, and then his credit card showed purchases here, on the docks." He looked sidewise to Andie.

"Ah, Pete," Andie said.

"Yeah, well, we haven't been able to catch up with him to ask what he knows about it. He's not always here when the store claims to be open," Sean said.

"Feel my pain," Andie muttered.

Stacy sifted through the papers. "This next one is for *Fin Fun Charters*," she said.

"That's Frankie's shop," Andie said. Given what had happened the night before, she was not surprised.

"So, you think one of these guys knows something about the missing diver? Do you have any idea what this has to do with Andie's dead patient? Is the guy from last night involved too?" Stacy asked.

Sean nodded and grabbed the papers back from her. Looking at them next to each other reminded Andie of a joke from high school. Stacy and Sean were the same height, and their complexions were similar. They used to pretend to be twins separated by divorce. It helped Stacy get close to his friends. Better said, it helped her to get dates with his friends.

"Yes, to all of that, but that's all I'm going to say about it right now," Sean said.

Stacy narrowed her eyes and scowled at him.

"Andie, since Pete's not here, can we start at *Fin Fun*?" Sean continued. "As you know, Frankie disappeared after the incident last night. I'm hoping he came in to work today."

They walked slowly down the docks, passing ice cream parlors and curio shops, where tourists were happily under-dressed for the chilly fall weather. Andie had to remember that for most of the country, a high of sixty-eight degrees in October meant it was time for shorts and a barbeque.

When they reached Frankie's store, the door was open but no one was inside. Andie walked in first and Sean followed closely behind. He started to look around. Frankie's store was neater than Pete's. He also carried more dive related items, such as clothing and hats; things that the tourists might be interested in. He had bumper stickers, shoes, and shot glasses, all bearing an image of the traditional SCUBA diver flag: a red background with a white stripe running diagonally across the middle. Andie had told Pete that he should cater more to the tourists, that he should sell souvenirs and items unique to Florida. He always told her that he was not going to sellout and cheapen the sport of SCUBA diving with tchotchkes and 'stupid shit like that.'

No wonder his shop sucks, Andie thought.

Stacy brushed her fingers over a brightly painted seashell wind chime, and the noise was eerie in the quiet dark of the empty shop. There was a fountain beverage sitting on the counter next to the cash register. The sweat from the ice ran down the plastic cup and created a small pool on the scratched plastic.

"Sean, someone's been here recently, the cup's still sweating and it hasn't spread far," Andie called to Sean, who had passed into the back room of the store.

"No one's back there, either," he said as he emerged through plastic strips that served as a barrier between the front and the back of the dive shop.

Stacy was wandering around looking at the merchandise. She walked behind a counter and started picking at what was back there. Andie smelled neoprene mixed with the scent of new clothing and it reminded her of the souvenir shops that littered the larger beach communities in the county. Again, she reflected on why Pete's shop was not as successful as Frankie's was.

"Look at this." Stacy pulled out a mess of folded paper and spread it out on a plexiglass case that displayed lighters and belt buckles.

"It's a topographic map of Florida," Andie pointed out. "Maybe a geological survey...?" The map had been unfolded and refolded multiple times; the creases were brown with nicotine and torn in places.

"What's all this?" Stacy asked. Sean bent in and looked closer at red lines and circles that had been drawn over the center of the state.

"I can't tell," he said.

Sean went back to the register and looked through drawers. He rifled through old papers and then flipped through a ragged address book. He picked up the old cordless phone and the women heard beeping as he scrolled through recent calls. He took out his note pad and scribbled something quickly.

"I'm going to get someone to look into a few things for me, I'll be right back." He walked out to the dock and made a call.

Andie and Stacy kept inspecting the ragged map. Sean had shut the door on his way out and the store was quiet. Not even the noise from the marina permeated the front window. Andie heard Stacy breathing as the tall blonde concentrated on the red markings.

The creek of a screen door interrupted their thoughts. Stacy and Andie looked up at the same time. They started towards the back room, towards the sound of the same screen door closing on its own. As they approached the plastic strips, they heard a series of metallic squeaking sounds. It sounded like someone opening an old faucet. Soon there was the rushing hiss of escaping gas.

The two women stopped and looked at each other. They stayed hidden, against the wall near the plastic tentacles that extended down from the top of the doorframe. Andie peered carefully around the corner and saw the silhouette of a man against the bright sun that streamed in through the open back door. The glare from the ally made it difficult for her to make out any other details.

Tink

The sound of a small metal hinge opening, the sound of thin brass on brass, cut through the hiss of the oxygen. It took a moment for the noise to register, and in that moment, Andie heard the sound of metal striking flint. There was no spark. Again, the flint wheel spun; still no ignition. As the third attempt to strike a flame came from the back room, Andie grabbed Stacy and dragged her towards the front door.

Her feet were painful and bulky. She stumbled as she felt the wounds on her feet re-open, and she fell to the carpet. Stacy picked her up and wrapped an arm around her waist. Together they bolted through the front door.

"Run!" Andie yelled to Sean, who was walking back from his car.

No sooner had they cleared the front of the store, they heard the explosion from inside of *Fin Fun Charters*. The front glass blew out and flew over the railing that Andie had vaulted the night before. Squares of safety glass rained like hail into the marina and Andie, Sean, and Stacy were thrown to the worn, wooden dock.

Chapter Eleven

With alarming déjà vu, Andie sat on the same wooden bench as the night before. A medic was tending to the new superficial wounds she sustained in the blast. Then, he said, he would redress the cuts on her feet, which had bled through the fresh gauze. She asked the guy who took care of her where Damian was.

"He was on the overnight; he won't be back on until tomorrow," he replied as he wrapped her feet in fluffy kerlex.

Andie's ears were ringing; she had abrasions on her knees and the palms of her hands from where she had hit the wood. Again, the medics wanted to take her to the ER, mostly for observation, they said. She was happy to see that Stacy was just as belligerent as she was about further care.

"I am just fine!" She heard Stacy yell at the girl who was trying to convince her to let them transport her to the hospital. "How old are you anyway? You look like you're thirteen. No offense sweetie, I'm just saying you look young. I bet you were still in pre-k while I was in anatomy class."

Andie laughed out loud and Stacy looked over at her.

"Right?" Stacy called to her. "Don't they look so young?"

Andie nodded. "We're just old, actually," she retorted. She signed the refusal paper being held out by the male medic. The girl medic held a similar one out for Stacy to sign.

"There you go," Stacy said, dotting the 'I's' in her last name forcefully.

After they were done, Sean had officers come and take their statements.

"Did you get a look at the guy?" they were both asked.

"No," Andie replied. "He was backlit by the open door. He was skinny though. It definitely was not Frankie."

It was well into the afternoon by the time they were done with the police questioning. Sean paced the scene the whole time, always keeping his eye trained on Andie. When they were finally done, all that Andie wanted was a hot bath.

"Do you want me to just take you home, or should I take you back to your car? Are you ok to drive?" Stacy asked.

"I can drive home. Just take me back to Cabanas, please."

Sean walked them to Stacy's sports car. He had mild scrapes on his face and hands, but otherwise was doing well for having been that close to an explosion. When they reached the red roadster, he pulled Andie aside. "I'm glad you're ok," he said.

Andie smiled and looked up, into his deep blue eyes. They were gentle, and they exposed his concern for her. Again, she felt uncomfortable with the intensity of his gaze. "Thanks," she responded.

Sean returned her smile. It was a disarming, boyish smile. Andie's heart beat faster.

"Come on you two, should I let y'all get a room? Or do you want to take her home yourself, Sean?" Stacy called across the top of the car.

"*Then ntrepesae*?! Don't be fresh." Andie chastised. "I'm ready, let's go."

Sean hovered until she was seated. He closed the door once she was settled.

"I'll call you," Sean said. Andie nodded.

She leaned back against the headrest. The roadster was low to the ground and Andie felt like she had been stuffed into the small seat. She could not believe this was the same car she had ridden over in.

I guess everything feels different after almost being blown up, she thought to herself.

The ring of the phone through the blue tooth was deafening and Andie jolted upright. She cursed as she jammed her feet into the floor reflexively. Pain surged through her already swollen feet. Stacy hit the phone button on her steering wheel.

"Hey, Aphrodite," she answered.

"Stacy, are you ok? Is Andie with you?" Aphrodite's voice sounded near panic.

"We're both here," Andie answered.

"Oh, thank God! I saw all of the police cars down town, and then I heard on the news there had been an explosion. Sean told me y'all just left the scene. Are you on your way to the hospital?"

They laughed.

"No, Aphrodite," Stacy answered, "don't talk crazy. I'm taking Andie to her car so she can go home, and then I have a hot tub with my name on it."

"That's it; I'm coming over to both of your houses." The call ended. Stacy and Andie looked at each other and then they both rolled their eyes. It wasn't long before the phone rang again. Stacy punched at the steering wheel for a second time.

"Yes Maria—we're both here, we're both alive, and we're not going to the hospital," Stacy said.

"*Ay Dios!*" Maria exclaimed. "Aphrodite made it sound like the whole dock went up in flames and took you two with it!"

"We're fine," Andie said.

She actually was not feeling that great, but as always 'fine' was relative. It's easy for someone to complain about a headache, but then when you are on an overnight shift in the hospital, and a migrant worker comes in with a worm in his brain from eating undercooked pork, the definition of 'headache' changes. So it was with 'fine.'

"Aphrodite says she's coming to check on you guys. Do I need to come, too?" Maria asked.

"No, really," Stacy said. "I promise I'll call you later to let you know I'm still alive, ok?"

"Sure, but make sure you call, seriously. I might not be a doctor, but I know what that kind of trauma can do to a person." Maria was first generation Cuban-American. Her parents had landed on the beach in South Florida when she was an infant. Her father had stories about trying to resist the dictatorship in Cuba, and Maria had grown up hearing all of the gory details, repeatedly.

"We promise," Andie said, looking at Stacy.

"Yeah, we promise."

***

"You know the signs of a concussion, so I'm sure you don't need my lecture," Stacy said as she pulled into the gravel driveway of The Cabana.

"Yeah, yeah. Plus, Aphrodite's coming over, remember? Look, call me later. I'll check on you, and you can check on me, deal? And don't forget to call Maria."

Stacy laughed. "No worries, I won't forget. Take care, sweetie."

They exchanged kisses on each cheek and Andie slowly climbed out of the sports car. She walked carefully over the stones in the parking lot. She watched Stacy drive away and then Andie looked out into the marina. She took in a deep breath and smiled at the familiar scent of salt water and fuel. She was feeling grateful to be alive, but since the explosion, she had been struggling with a repeated rapid replay of the whole event in her mind. She remembered everything: the smell of the store, the sound of the lighter, the explosion. She couldn't stop hearing the explosion. She couldn't stop feeling the pressure wave as it struck her back. It struck like a falling tree, forcing her to the rough splinter-filled ground. It had been so real, so solid. Andie tried again to clear her mind. She directed her thoughts back to the old topographical map.

Where had they gone diving? she thought. She wished she still had the tattered document. She tried her best to recall the image; she closed her eyes and pictured the map on the display case. But all she kept seeing was the outline of the man. She heard the clink of the lighter, and then felt the splintered wood where she lay face down on the dock.

She took in a deep breath and shook her head. She concentrated on enjoying the smell of the sea; she looked out at the boats again. As she strained her eyes against the late afternoon sun, she noticed a man walking quickly down the main dock. He was carrying a duffle bag, and something about him was familiar. His silhouette. His silhouette against the hazy sky was unmistakable.

Andie moved as quickly as she could, trying not to open her wounds again. She walked towards the marina gates, attempting to stay hidden behind an outcropping of sea grapes that grew close to the water. She watched as the man with the bag boarded an old, broken-down boat.

He was skinny; he had dark hair and he was wearing sunglasses. He moved quickly and when he took off his glasses, Andie recognized his face. It was the man she had rescued from the water. Andie watched as he donned a thick wetsuit and pulled on a tank. He looked around and Andie ducked behind the foliage. There was a distant splash, and when she looked back, he was gone. All that she saw was a ripple in the cloudy harbor water where he had gone under.

Andie hobbled to the marina office.

"Hey there, I'm wondering if you can tell me whose boat that is down there?" she asked.

The teenage dock attendant, who had been wholly captivated by his phone, looked up slowly.

"The one that looks like it needs to be repaired," Andie continued. "No, not the blue one, the one two down...yeah, that one."

He gazed blankly at her for a moment before responding to her inquiry.

"Uh...some guy, I think," he said.

"Really? Some guy, huh? Wow, thanks," Andie responded.

He must know Kallie, she thought as she left the small shack.

She walked out on to the dock, wondering how much time she had before the skinny man surfaced. She moved closer and took a picture of the boat, trying to ensure that she was not too close in case she needed to get away quickly. Andie zoomed her phone's camera in so that she could see the name of the boat and the registration that was printed on the side of the hull.

She snapped a few photos and when she looked up, she saw the man's head come out of the water. She pretended to be taking pictures of a nearby boat that had a 'for sale' sign on it. She quickly pocketed her phone and headed back to shore. She didn't dare to look over her shoulder in case he noticed her. She strolled off the dock as casually as she could, and then hurried gingerly back to her car.

Chapter Twelve

"Officer Malone here," Sean answered.

"Sean, hey, it's Andie."

"Are you ok? Why are you calling my work phone? Did you make it home ok?"

"Relax, I'm fine. And this is official business, so I called your work phone, and no, I'm not home yet, but I'm on my way."

"Ok, do you need help? Where are you?"

"Sean, I'm fine, calm down. I'm almost home. Stacy brought me back to my car, and as I was getting ready to drive home I saw the guy... it was the guy I pulled out of the water last night. And..." she flashed back to the silhouette in the back room of *Fin Fun Charters*. "...I'm fairly sure it was the same guy who caused the explosion. He's at the marina near The Cabana."

"Ok, good. Did you approach him?"

"No," Andie said. The weight of the last couple of days was laying heavy on her mind, but she had not lost all common sense. "I was almost blown up today, and then I see the guy who likely did it? I'm not approaching him, don't worry."

"Good. Where are you now?"

"Turning on to my street. I need a shower and some ice cream."

"I'll meet you there," Sean said. The call ended before Andie could say no.

***

When she got home, Sean was sitting on the front steps of the old Key West style house that Andie had bought after the divorce. She was suddenly conscious of the landscaping, happy that the guy who took care of her lawn had been there the day before. He did a great job of keeping the grass green, the palm trees healthy, and the weeds from invading the plant beds that ran along the ground in front of the porch.

The porch stretched across the entire front of the house. It extended equally in both directions from the three steps that led up to the heavy front doors. There was a hanging bench swing on one side, and a pair of wicker chairs on the other. Andie put her personal touch to the idyllic picture with a side table made by a local artist. It was a wooden mermaid holding up a piece of round glass. It lived between the two white wicker chairs.

Sean was dressed in a fresh dress-casual outfit. He sat, smiling, with the double wooden front doors as a backdrop. Stacy was right, he was looking very good.

Andie was stiff as she climbed out of her car. The door creaked and popped in its comforting way as it swung shut. She stepped carefully on the flagstone walk that led from the driveway to the front steps. She was conscious of Sean watching her as she made her way to him and wished she could move faster. She groaned as she lowered herself down next to him.

"I am so sore," Andie stated. "How are you? Or are you used to being blown up?" Their arms were touching and Andie did not move to change that.

"A little, where I hit the dock. Other than sore, how're you doing?" He put an arm around her. The weight on her shoulders was comforting. She leaned in to him and rested her head on his shoulder. She felt a jolt of unexpected excitement as she breathed in his clean, masculine scent. After a pause she responded, "I'm stiff, and my feet hurt." She paused again. "And I must admit that I'm a little scared."

"I know how much you hate saying that," he said with a smile. He rubbed her arm. "And along that line, I need to send some officers out to the marina, so what information can you give me?"

Andie showed him the photos of the boat. He got up and walked to the end of the driveway, still holding her phone.

Andie watched as he paced near the street during his call. For a guy who had been near an explosion, he looked exceptionally well put together. He had the sleeves of his fresh dress shirt rolled up to his elbows, exposing his tan forearms. Andie noted once again that his black belt matched his worn, but clean shoes. He smiled when he saw her watching him. He finished his call and then came back.

"They're on their way now," Sean said as he sat down again. Andie nodded.

"I'm going to go take a shower," she said. Sean stood up with her as she got ready to go inside. He stayed at the bottom of the stairs as she reached the door, his hands resting casually on his hips.

"Do you want me to post someone outside, on the street?" he asked.

Andie thought about it.

"Nah, I'm ok. Thanks, though. I've got Athena."

Sean stayed and watched Andie until the door was locked. He glanced over his shoulder only once as he walked back to his car.

***

Andie did not go running the next morning. In fact, her feet were so sore that she spent the time before church with ice packs strapped to the soles of her feet. Her legs were propped up on the ottoman and she was eating a bowl of Cheerios® while flipping through television channels. The ace bandages wrapped around the ice to keep the packs from falling off were just starting to moisten when Kallie came and squeezed between her and Athena.

"You ok, Mom?" she asked.

"I'm good, baby. How are you?" Andie put her cereal on the side table and snaked her arm around Kallie's shoulder.

Kallie shrugged. "I'm fine."

"Do you want to talk, honey?" Andie asked.

Kallie stared at the floor sullenly. "Not really. Do we have to go to Yaya's for dinner tonight?"

Andie squeezed her. "No, *hara mou*, we don't have to go. How about we just come home and order Chinese food and watch a trashy movie?"

Kallie was still staring at the floor, but she managed a smile. "Sure. But I'm picking the movie, because all of your movie choices suck."

"I love you, too!" Andie called after Kallie as she went to her room to get ready for church.

Andie's bandaged feet did not fit in any church-appropriate footwear. She ended up in her sports slides, but still she moved slowly. She tried her best to hurry, but she and Kallie were late to church nonetheless. Holy Trinity was large enough, however, that their appearance at the back of the chapel went mostly unnoticed. They went up the side aisle and snuck into the pew beside Andie's mother.

"*Pouisoum*?" her mother whispered.

"*Asehmeh*, let it go, Ma. I know we're late, shhh," Andie replied with a hiss. She didn't think that now was the time to tell her mother about the explosion the day before.

"Petros was on time," her mother continued. She leaned back and Andie saw Pete on her other side. He smiled his typical chauvinistic smile. Andie wished murder wasn't frowned upon in the house of God.

She had to wait until after the service to talk to him about what happened on the docks.

"You didn't tell my mom, did you?" she asked.

He shook his head. "And be the cause of her heart attack? Don't be crazy."

"I hate it when you call me crazy," Andie said.

"I'm not calling you crazy!"

Andie stood with her arms crossed, staring off at the table that held the regular after church assortment of coffee and pastries. Kallie was chatting with friends nearby.

"Sorry," she finally said. "I guess I'm a little sensitive."

"Yeah, you are."

"God, Pete! I was apologizing, that's not the freaking time to be self-righteous! I'm so glad we're divorced."

He put an arm around her shoulder and stood next to her smiling. "We're not divorced, remember?"

"Oh, yeah, my mother never lets me forget." She shrugged Pete's arm off of her shoulders.

"Speaking of..." Pete said.

Andie watched her small mother cross the room towards them.

"Petro, are you coming to dinner tonight?" she asked.

Sophia cupped Andie's face in her hands. Andie tried to hide her annoyance with a kind smile. It took everything she had not to pull away.

"He's not coming to dinner tonight," Andie said.

"Yes, thank you, Sophia, I would love to," Pete interjected.

Andie couldn't handle her frustration any longer.

"No, he's not." She took her mom's hands in hers and held them in front of her. "Mom, there was an explosion yesterday, at the docks. I'm still sore, and I'm not really in the mood for a family dinner with my ex-husband."

"Husband," her mother corrected.

Andie drew in a breath through her nose and blew it out through her mouth. "My point is..." She proceeded to relay the story of the explosion to her mother. The information began a whole new episode of her mother touching her. She examined Andie's head, her shoulders, arms, back, even her backside.

"Ma, I'm fine!" Andie finally said. "The medics checked me out, nothing is broken."

"You should see a doctor," her mother said sternly.

"Ma, I *am* a doctor."

Her mother waved dismissively.

"I know, I know, but *kore mou*, you cannot always care for yourself."

"Sure Ma, I'll see a doctor." She could tell that her mother didn't believe her, but she dropped the issue.

"*Keh Kaliope mou!* So beautiful! I have the car all clean and ready for her birthday, so whenever you are ready for it, let me know."

"We'll see," Andie said. She had been saying the same words since Kallie got her driver's permit months earlier.

Andie felt her pocket vibrate and excused herself.

"Stacy?" she said as she answered her phone. "It's Sunday, what's up?" Everyone knew that Andie was off limits during church hours.

"I know, I'm sorry, but I wanted to let you know that Sean searched the boat you saw and found some interesting information."

"Ok..." Andie said, still not comprehending why this was urgent.

"It looks like the boat belonged to Frankie. Police found receipts on the boat, though, and gear from *Sun and Fun Scuba*."

Andie ended the call and marched back into the communion hall. She grabbed Pete's elbow and forced him outside.

"Ow!" he exclaimed.

"Suck it up. We need to talk."

Chapter Thirteen

"Look, you slimy bastard, if you weren't involved than tell me what you know!" Andie was pacing in front of her car, outside of the church. She was so upset that she did not even notice the pain in her feet.

"I'm telling you, I don't know anything about it!" Pete said, for what must have been the fourth time.

"You were just miraculously gone during business hours yesterday? And don't think I've forgotten you missed the hand off on Friday night. And don't-" she interrupted his protestations, "Don't tell me you had students."

"Fine," he admitted. "There was a rush cleaning job, ok?"

Pete's pride led him to do everything he could to hide what his real job was. The dive shop and teaching SCUBA to tourists didn't bring in enough to earn him a living. His real paying job, the job that made everything else possible, was cleaning barnacles off the bottoms of other people's boats.

Andie put her head down and pinched the bridge of her nose. She sighed.

"You just had to tell me, Pete. Really, just be honest with me. And Kallie, be honest with her. How do you think it made her feel that you weren't there when I tried to drop her off?"

"I know, I know," Pete said. He turned around and faced the church. "I'm a horrible father."

Andie knew what he was waiting for, but she wasn't going to argue with this statement. She changed the subject back to the explosion.

"Pete, they found gear from your store in the boat that a suspect in the bombing was using. It's Frankie's boat, Pete. What's your stuff doing on Frankie's boat?"

"I honestly don't know," he responded with his hands in the air.

"Well you better come up with something, because the police have been looking for you and I'm sure they will be more insistent on getting an answer than I am."

***

Sean arrived at Markos Family Medicine mid-morning the next day. Andie found him waiting in the hall as she was coming out of a patient room. He was strolling casually along the tiled floor, looking at Andie's diplomas that were artfully arranged on the wall. Andie had nothing to do with this. Her decorating style was more old-world junk chic, or, as her daughter once described it, like an antique shop gave Andie all of its rejects. So, when it came to decorating, Dr. Markos left it up to her capable staff to ensure that the office was presentable and welcoming.

"Just see Lupé and she will get you your lab script and set you up for your follow up appointment," Andie finished saying to her patient as she closed the door. She motioned Sean to follow her as she carefully strode to her office. She was in her sport-slides again. The only thing they remotely matched was scrubs, so Andie had donned the blue pajama-like outfit after her shower that morning.

She sat down and started typing up the patient's note on her computer and when Sean didn't start speaking, she stopped and looked at him.

"Go ahead," she said.

"Go ahead, what?" he said.

"Talk, tell me whatever you're here for," she said, looking back to her work.

"What, you're going to keep working?"

Fingers still on the keyboard Andie turned and stared at him. "Unless you're going to tell me that this is official police business and I have to give you my full attention, then yes, I'm going to keep working." She turned her attention once more to her monitor.

"Sure, ok…" Sean stammered. "I wanted-"

Stella poked her head in the door and interrupted.

"Three months or three weeks for Mr. Yanikakis?" she asked.

"I put three months," Andie responded, still typing. Stella didn't say anything. Andie stopped and looked at her. "Didn't I…?" Stella shook her head and bit her lip.

"You clicked the 'three weeks' button. But no problem," added Stella quickly. "I'll just tell Lupé three months. Can you just, um, can you fix it in the computer before you sign the note?"

"Of course," Andie said. She rolled her eyes and groaned. She called after her Medical Assistant, "The groan was not for you Stella!"

"I know, doc," she heard Stella reply as she moved back towards the front desk.

"I hate stinking electronic health records," Andie said. She turned from her computer and sighed. Now facing Sean, she clasped her hands together and rested them on the desk. "Since I'm boycotting the computer for the moment, go ahead."

"Who knew doctors had to be computer savvy?" Sean said.

Andie snorted sardonically. "Certainly no one in med school. But I don't want to talk about that, tell me what you came to tell me."

"Are you sure I can talk now?" Sean asked.

"Very funny. Yes, go ahead."

He pulled out his notepad.

"We found-"

"Pete's stuff on the boat, I know," Andie interrupted.

Sean cleared his throat.

"A lock box attached to the anchor of Frankie's boat is what I was going to say. And yes, we did find some gear from Pete's store on the boat as well. What is up with you, Andie?"

Andie knuckles turned white as she tightened her grip on herself. She looked down at her desk and then back up at Sean.

"I'm at work," she stated simply. "I have three rooms, two are full, and Stella is putting another patient in the third one. I am already thirty minutes behind, which is actually really good for me, but the longer I sit here the further behind I get. I have ten open notes, over one hundred tasks, which could easily be someone's abnormal mammogram or scan, and it's Monday, so I'm trying to catch up on all of my patients who went to the ER over the weekend. My ears hurt, my feet are killing me, and my shoulder has an amazingly beautiful ecchymosis, ugg." She dropped her face into her hands momentarily, remembering that not everyone wanted to hear doctor-speak in regular conversation. "Sorry, a <u>bruise</u> that has bloomed over the last forty-eight hours. I had a near-death experience, saw a shady guy get on a run-down boat that wasn't even his, on which there was evidence that links my ex-husband to this whole craziness. Actually, that last part I don't mind so much. But my point is: I'm tired, I have patients to see, tasks to do, and when I'm here, and in doctor mode, it's all solution, all the time. So, let's get down to business in the fewest words possible, okay?"

Sean's eyes widened. "Shall I come back later?" he asked.

"That would, um, actually be the best idea," Andie said as she stood up.

Stella stuck her head in through the office door again.

"Three's ready for you, but room two is first," she said.

"Thanks, I'll be right there," Andie said. She ushered Sean out of her office and pulled the door closed behind her.

***

That night as she was leaving the office, Andie got a text from Sean.

"Better time now?" he wrote.

"Sure," she responded. "Come by."

He was there when she got home. She pulled out her phone and sent him a text from her car.

"U were here, weren't you?"

He looked at her from the stairs and smiled.

"Yup," he texted back.

She was putting her phone in her bag when she felt it vibrate again. This time it was a text from Kallie.

"The red head guy is here."

"So am I. Coming in now," she responded.

Andie walked past Sean where he was now standing at the bottom of the front stairs.

"Can we go in and chat?" she asked, as she brushed past him on her way up the stairs. She opened the door and turned around to let him follow her. Athena jumped on him and stuck her nose in his ear. He laughed and scratched her head.

"Athena, no, off!" Andie commanded. The dog jogged back to the living room and took up her place on the leather couch.

Once the door was closed, Andie pointed to the living room, "You have a seat, and I'll be right back."

Andie put her stuff on the coat rack and went to her room to change. When she came back to talk to Sean she was in a much better mood.

"So, what did they find?" she asked. She handed Sean one of the glasses of ice water that she held and then sat down next to Athena.

"A waterproof lock box," he said.

He handed two glossy photographs to Andie. The top one was an old looking rusty dagger on a white background, lined up next to black rulers. It was the second picture however, that was the most intriguing.

"What is this?" she asked after inspecting the image.

"Burned plastic. The burned driver's license of our missing person, actually." Sean took the photos back. He leaned back in his armchair and put the ice water down on the side table. He wiped his hands on his pants.

"I would offer you something stronger, but I know you're working," Andie said.

"Yeah," Sean said absently. She could see that he was tired, that, try as he might, the last few days were getting to him as well.

"So, this skinny guy, the guy I rescued, is linked to your missing person?" Andie continued.

"It's a little deeper than that," Sean admitted.

He told her about searching the missing diver's home. "Like I told you already, when the police in Pennsylvania searched his house they found receipts for dive gear. There was also evidence that he had recently purchased equipment to go camping. When we went through his email account, there were lots of emails between him and three other guys. The three other divers were here, in Florida. It seems like they were planning a dive trip somewhere here in this state.

"Since we never found his body, we had to assume he was still alive, but then we found this," he held up the picture of the burned driver's license. "Why would someone burn his ID? And then, why would they keep it, hide it, unless they wanted to make sure he stayed missing?"

Andie nodded.

"And this is where you come in. One of the guys in the emails was your dead patient. The third was his dive partner, the one who died in Wild Boar Springs. As you know, there was evidence of a struggle and the suggestion of foul play on their last dive together. So that night when I paged you, we were headed to Anthony Siegel's house to question him about all of this. And then we found him dead, too."

Andie put the time line together in her head. "So, the last diver in their team is the only one still alive, or at least possibly alive? Who is he?"

"We know his name, but he hasn't been back to his place in Tampa since we found your patient dead."

Andie sat thoughtfully as she processed this information. "So, let me ask you," she asked, leaning forward. "Why are you telling me all of this? I'm not a cop."

Sean sighed and rubbed his temples. "Andie, I need to find Pete."

"Pete? Are you really going through me to get to Pete?"

"Look, it's just that we couldn't find him—he hasn't been home all weekend, and we thought you would know where he might be. Obviously, Frankie is involved in some way, and we can't find him either. Pete's our only available connection at this time. I have to find him. If he has nothing to do with this, then at least he might be able to point us in the right direction. He's a technical diver, he's in that crowd. He might know something."

"I can't decide if I should call you an asshole or not," Andie said.

"Call me what you want to," Sean said. His voice became more official. "But Pete might know something. Andie, this is a murder investigation. Murder. And this thing here?" He held up the picture of the knife. "It dates back to the 1600's. It's Spanish, like conquistador Spanish.

What was our mystery man doing with this? I mean, people have killed for far less than buried treasure. And where is our missing diver? We have his burned license, which is fishy, obviously. And where is Frankie, can you tell me? Because I don't know, and I'm trying to find out, so I'm looking to talk to Pete to see if he might know anything, anything at all."

"Annoying when someone messes with your work."

"Oh my God, yes. You are being annoying right now," Sean said. He got up and walked towards the front door.

"So are you," Andie retorted childishly. She followed him into the front hall. "Sean, all you had to do was ask if I knew where Pete was, because I would gladly have told you. I actually would have paid money to watch him be taken aside by the police at church yesterday."

Sean chuckled.

Again, Andie noted how tired he looked. Andie could see that he was serious about solving this murder and she felt bad for giving him a hard time. She stretched and yawned.

"He would kill me for telling you this, but you can find him at the boat house near the Sponge Dock Marina most mornings, around seven. He cleans boats there." She walked to the door to see him out.

"Thanks," Sean said as he passed between Andie and the coat rack. He stopped before he was fully out of the door.

The space between the open door and the coat rack was small, and Andie could feel his heat as he stepped closer to her. He leaned down and brushed her cheek softly with his lips. Andie didn't realize her eyes were closed until he pulled away. She cursed herself for being caught off guard.

"I'll call you tomorrow," he said with a smile that crinkled the corners of his blue eyes. Andie nodded. Her emotions were too tumultuous for her to formulate a verbal response.

Both of them were so distracted that they didn't see the old truck that had been parked just within sight of the house. They didn't hear the truck drive slowly past; they didn't see the skinny man who noted their closeness, who watched the whole exchange, who saw the kiss.

Chapter Fourteen

Stacy called Andie on the way into work the next morning.

"Did Sean tell you about the knife?" Stacy asked. "Kind of cool, right?"

"Yeah," Andie responded. "But for some reason that makes this whole thing feel more, I don't know, dangerous."

"This is murder Andie," Stacy said with a laugh. "Of course it's dangerous."

"Look, you might see the result of violence every day, but the most dangerous my day gets is when I deny someone their narcs or benzos. Or when someone comes in with a positive PPD, then I have to get the health department involved."

"Speaking of which, have you gotten your lab work back from your exposure that night on the dock?"

Since the mystery man she had rescued was bleeding when Andie gave him mouth-to-mouth, she had to do serial testing for blood-borne diseases.

"Yeah, so far so good. But you know the drill, I'll keep checking, and I won't really feel safe until the twelve-month check."

"I completely understand. But seriously, back to the treasures. Have you heard anything from Pete?"

"Jesus! Really, you too?" Andie hit the brakes harder than intended and the car behind her honked. She raised her hand in apology.

"What?! I'm just wondering if he knows anything about it, that's all. This is lost *treasure*, Andie. That's like every Floridians secret wish—to find ancient Spanish treasure."

"It's just that Sean already grilled me on this."

"Oh, he 'grilled you,' did he? Is that what we're calling it these days?"

"You're like a twelve-year-old boy. You need to get laid," Andie said as she turned into her office parking lot.

"Oh, so true," Stacy responded.

Andie was silent. She pulled into her parking space and switched off the car. She picked up her phone as the call went from Bluetooth back to the handset.

"Andie? You still there?" asked Stacy. "I was just kidding about Sean."

"Yeah, I'm here. I know."

"Are you ok, honey?"

Andie paused again. She was fine with being vulnerable with her friends; she had no problem talking about her feelings. Except when she was at work. When she was at work, she was in business mode and focused more on solving the problems around her, not those going on inside of her.

"I'm ok. I'm just feeling a little put off by seeing Sean so much recently. And then," she rubbed her eyes with her spare hand. "He kissed me last night."

"What?? Yay!!" Stacy paused. When Andie didn't respond she added, "Or not yay…?"

"No, it's ok, I mean it's good, I think." Andie smiled, remembering the feeling of him so close. She could remember his smell, clean yet masculine. "But I have this weird feeling in my gut…"

"That means you need to take him to your bedroom and take his clothes off," Stacy said.

Andie heard the bone saw screech to life in the background.

"Stacy, I mean a different feeling," Andie laughed. "I don't know, I'm just uneasy."

"Well," Stacy said. The saw started to cut through an unknown body part and Stacy raised her voice. "Just make sure you call your red-headed cop friend and have him come take care of you."

"Funny. And I can hear your day has started. I'm sitting outside my office, I have to go in," Andie said. She got out and walked to the passenger side of her car; she took out her work bag and started towards the back door.

"Ok, don't kill anyone, because I don't need the extra work," Stacy said.

"And you, don't make any wrong calls on your posts, I'm sure your colleagues don't need the extra work either," Andie retorted.

"Shut up," Stacy chuckled.

"Love you," Andie said as the call ended.

***

Athena greeted Andie at the door as usual when she got home that night. Kallie was watching television in the living room.

"Is your homework done?" Andie asked as she hung up her bag.

"Uh huh," Kallie said without looking up.

"So, if I go in your backpack and read your agenda I will see that you have done everything?"

"I'm not ten anymore Mom, I have a planner now, not an agenda."

"Well sorry, little Ms. Sophisticated." Andie walked into the kitchen and took out leftovers from the night before.

"I'm glad you're feeling better," Kallie called from the living room.

Andie chuckled as she put leftover Chinese food in the microwave for dinner. Florida was like the Bermuda Triangle for Chinese food-the best anyone could ever hope for from Chinese takeout restaurants in their area was for it to be consistently mediocre. Andie went to her room and changed into pajamas.

Kallie was more talkative at dinner than normal. Andie didn't mind. She tried to ask enough questions to keep her daughter talking, but not so many that Kallie would realize she was divulging actual information about her life.

"And so apparently Jordan told Sam that we were going to the Winter Formal together, but he hasn't asked me yet," concluded Kallie.

"Winter Formal?" Andie said with surprise. "But it's only October. And you're still a junior!"

"But Jordan's a senior, Mom. Duh."

"Oh my God, how could I be so stupid?! Ugg, you must hate having such a dumb mother! How did I even make it through med school?"

Kallie rolled her eyes, but smiled.

"Kallie, you know how I feel about this. You're too young. No Winter Formal for you."

"Mom! I'm going to be sixteen. You met dad in high school."

"And look how that turned out?!" Andie sighed and reached over to smooth Kallie's hair out of her face. She looked so much like her father, but even with this constant reminder of the mistakes of her younger years, Andie had never loved anything or anyone as much as she loved her daughter.

"Do we get to go shopping for a dress then?" Andie finally asked.

Kallie squealed and clapped her hands, but then her face became serious.

"Well, see..." Kallie started.

"Ah, yeah, so now here's The Thing... come on, tell me The Thing."

"The thing is," Kallie continued, "that Shana said there is a really big dress sale tonight in Tampa, and it's only going on tonight.... Can I go? Please?"

Andie wanted to keep Kallie safe; she wanted to keep her inside for the rest of her life so that nothing could happen to her, ever. At the same time, however, Andie was culturally susceptible to spoiling her only child. She didn't have to think very long before she answered.

"Of course, *hara mou*. But make sure your dad's friends don't see you out-they will tell your dad, who will call your grandmother..." They both rolled their eyes. Andie continued, "And sniff sniff, I kinda want to be there when you buy your formal dress."

"What if we go together next year to pick out the dress for my Senior Prom?" Kallie offered.

"Pinky promise?" Andie held up her outstretched little finger. Kallie linked her pinky with her mother's.

"I pinky promise."

Chapter Fifteen

Andie agreed to help Sean find Pete, but he had to wait until the end of the week. That Friday, Sean went to the *Sun and Fun SCUBA* early to meet Andie and Kallie, and to interview Pete. When he arrived, the door was propped open to let in the cool afternoon air. Pete was busy talking to a young, attractive blonde in tight pants and fur-lined boots.

"…The fire-ball was HUGE! The blast shook the whole dock. I'm lucky I survived, really," Sean heard him saying. Pete was leaning against the dirty display counter. Supporting his weight with one elbow, he reached up and twirled a lock of the blonde's hair. She noticed Sean first and pulled away.

Pete straightened up.

"Officer Sean McIrishman, what can I do for you on this fine October afternoon?"

Sean forced a smile. He strolled around the shop, gazing behind fixtures and in boxes. He touched an old oxygen tank on display and then had to wipe his hands on his pants to get rid of the dust that he got on his fingers.

"Petros Spanakopita, glad to see you hard at work."

The blonde shifted uncomfortably. "Well, Pete, thanks. I'll think about the lessons." She picked up her colorful beach bag and put it over her shoulder. She exited the store quickly.

"A student?" Sean commented with a jerk of his head in the direction of the door.

"What do you want, Sean?" Pete asked. He walked behind the counter and spread his arms out, palms flat on the yellowing plexiglass.

"I have some questions for you, that's all." Sean's phone sounded from his pocket. He looked at the text message and smiled. He typed a quick reply. "And I'm meeting Andie here when she drops of Kallie."

Pete stiffened at the mention of his ex-wife. He shook his head and sneered.

"You never could mind your own business," he said.

Sean shrugged. "Maybe not, but this time, this really is my business."

The two men stood in charged silence until Andie and Kallie arrived. Kallie greeted Sean and went to sit in the cluttered corner. Andie thought Pete's head was going to pop off when Kallie said hi to Sean first.

"Are you sending your pocket police man to keep an eye on me?" Pete spat.

"No, Pete, he has his own reason for being here," Andie replied. She carefully pulled over a dusty box and sat down next to her daughter. "Go ahead, Sean."

Sean turned to Pete with a smile. He opened the file he was holding.

"Do you know these men?" Sean laid four photos on top of the case.

Pete didn't look at them. "No," he said flatly.

"You have to look at them, Pete," Sean said. When Pete didn't answer, Sean smacked his hand down hard onto the scratched counter. "Look at the pictures!" he yelled. "This one," he picked up the picture of the missing diver and held it close to Pete's sneering face, "is missing, presumed dead. This one," he picked up the photo of Ross, "is dead. He died in a cave. This one," he picked up the picture of Anthony, "is dead. He died of tetanus. Yes, tetanus, which he got from this knife." Sean pulled out the picture of the artifact.

Pete's eyes became wide, like a child on Christmas morning. His mouth opened slightly as he slowly looked the photos over. Sean continued,

"And this guy?" He picked up the picture of the skinny man, "is missing. But the last place he was seen was on a boat that had your gear on it, a boat owned by your competition down the block, which also happens to be missing." Sean pointed towards the remains of *Fin Fun Charters,* his eyes never leaving Pete's face. "Oh, and he was seen on that boat after he blew up said competition. So, Mr. Markos, stop being such a childish little shit and look at the photos."

By the time he was done with his monologue, he was inches from Pete's round nose. The two men stared at each other, neither flinching. Eventually Pete put down the photograph of the knife and picked up the images of the men. Sean stepped back and crossed his arms in front of his chest.

Andie's heart was pounding. She had never seen Sean aggressive. All through high school he had been kind, sometimes to a fault. This was what ultimately broke them up--Sean said yes to everyone, and Andie just couldn't take it. But now, watching him as he worked... she liked this new Sean; the forceful edge made him so attractive.

"Yeah, actually, I think I do know them," Pete said finally. He handed the pile of photos back to Sean. "They came into my store looking to rent gear. This one," he pointed to the picture of Ross, "didn't need anything except to fill his tanks. We got to chatting and they told me they were going into a sinkhole somewhere. They were kind of dodgy about it, so I asked them for their cave certification. When only two of them could produce their credentials, I refused to fill their tanks. I'm not gonna be part of killing some stupid tourist who thinks an underground spring would be 'fun.'"

Sean glanced over at Andie and put the pictures away. She nodded.

"So how did they get your gear?" he asked.

"I'm assuming you're talking about the gear that was on Frankie's boat? Look, the only thing I can think of is that the gear you found was some I leant Frankie a long time ago. I honestly don't know how it got on his boat, and that's the truth."

Sean looked at Andie again and, again, she nodded. Pete leaned around him and looked at Andie as well.

"What, you gotta get her approval?" Pete sneered.

"No, it's just that I have years of knowing when you are lying," Andie answered.

Pete huffed and sat down on his cracked and rusting stool.

"Another question Pete, have you seen Frankie?" Sean asked.

"Not since the fire," he answered. His voice was forced and his face was sullen.

Andie could tell he was itching to start a fight with Sean. "Is that it, Officer Malone? I have business to attend to."

"No, that's not it, there's one more thing," Sean said. "Where have you been? We've been trying to reach you—I'm sure you've gotten my phone messages. I just want to make sure that we can find you if we need to."

"I have a life you know," Pete said. "Other than the store I mean." He looked surly. Andie could tell that it was killing him, but eventually he said, "But if you need me I promise that I will return your phone calls, okay? And don't worry, I won't leave town."

***

Pete was unusually quiet at church that Sunday. He did not make a single sexual overture towards Andie, and at Sophia's on Sunday afternoon, he refrained from trying to kiss her. Andie was not sure if it was the fear of the police or the fear of her being in a new relationship that was making him behave, but she didn't care as long as it continued.

She also did not hear from Sean for the rest of the weekend. They had only shared that one kiss, but she found herself looking at her phone, hoping that he might text her. Monday came and went without any contact. She started feeling ignored and jilted, so when she got his text in the middle of the week she was hesitant to respond.

"Got a min?" he wrote.

She was at work when the text came in. Her rooms were full and she really did not have the time for any kind of communication. She wasn't sure how to respond so she simply wrote,

"Not now."

When she didn't get an immediate response, she went to see her next patient. It wasn't until the end of the day that she had another moment to sit down and look at her phone. She found three new texts from Sean:

"When?"

"After work?"

And finally: "U call me then."

Needy men, Andie thought with annoyance. She had a passing moment acknowledging her own feelings from the weekend. She reflected on her own excitement at the thought of him contacting her, and then her disappointment when he didn't. These thoughts did not help her mood at all.

Andie had worked hard to become clear about her priorities: Kallie, work, her mother... ok, perhaps her friends came before her mother. But she knew that she didn't have space for someone else she had to take care of. Being a mom and a doctor was draining enough without having a man-child insisting that she devote her entire attention to him at the drop of a hat.

But she could not deny how she felt when she was close to him. His smell alone triggered a chemical reaction in her, a reaction that led her to want more of him. This desire, this primal drive to want to be near him again only annoyed her more.

Feelings suck, she thought.

She was sitting at her desk. The staff had gone home already and she was alone. The silence was wonderful, and the not having to answer sixteen questions at the same time was even better. She leaned back in her leather desk chair and closed her eyes. She let herself dive into her feelings a tiny bit. If she thought too much about them she would start to wallow, to get lost in the circular morass of the unexplained that lived in her head. If she continued to ignore them, however, she would continue to be irritated and irrational.

"God dammit," she said out loud. She re-settled herself into her chair. It was so much easier telling other people what to do than it was dealing with her own situations.

Maybe, she told herself, as her internal scale attempted to balance all of her thoughts on the situation. *Maybe I am being too hard on him. Maybe I am being too hard on myself.* Either way she felt irritated about her evolving feelings for Sean.

"Forget it," she said, opening her eyes and standing up. "Romance sucks. Work sucks. Everything sucks." She grabbed her bag and locked the office as she left.

She realized she needed to call Sean back, so before she pulled out of her parking space, she dialed his number. A rusty truck pulled into the line waiting to leave the parking lot. The skinny man behind the wheel kept his eyes on Andie's bumper.

"Sorry to bother you at work, I know you're busy," he began when he picked up. That made Andie smile; just these simple words erased her irritation at the interruption. Either that or hearing his voice settled her disappointment at his not contacting her over the weekend. She shook her head, pushing her feelings to the back of her mind again.

"What's up?" she asked.

"Do you remember that map at Frankie's place?"

"Of course. Watch it!" Andie screamed as the car in front of her came to a complete stop before making a left-hand turn. The truck behind her also stopped suddenly.

The "Snowbirds" had started coming back to Florida for the winter. This meant that individuals who lived half of the year in other parts of the country, generally northern states like Michigan, New York, and Ohio, were returning so they could spend the winter months in the balmy Florida climate. It also meant that the roads were more crowded, and that Andie had to practice more patience while driving. Given her heightened emotional state, patience was not as easily available as it normally was.

"Sorry," she apologized.

"Snowbirds?" asked Sean. She heard him laugh.

"Yeah. I try to remember that someday that will be me and I'll want people to have patience with me. But still, who comes to a complete stop when they take a left-hand turn?"

"Road rage kills you know."

"Oh, I know. Do you know how many drivers' licenses I have to take away? Doing that is harder than telling someone they have cancer."

It was part of Andie's job to let the Department of Motor Vehicles know if a person was not fit to be on the road any longer. It was one of the toughest things that she ever had to do. She knew that sometimes, if they couldn't drive, a patient might not have any other way to get food, or to even make it to see their doctor. It was even worse when she knew that they did not have any family nearby, and that without a driver's license they were more likely to sit at home, alone. Still, it was better than hearing about one of her patients killing a young kid on the road when she knew she might have been able to prevent it.

"And we here at the TSPD thank you for doing your part in keeping the streets safe."

"I'm sure you didn't ask me to call so we could talk about old people driving," Andie said.

"No, yeah, you're right. Look, that map--we think we might know what it was showing. We made it through Anthony Siegel's emails, and the last email between him and the missing diver says that they got a camping site in Brooksville, and they would go out from there. Is there a dive spot near there?"

"Plenty," Andie responded. "Cold Springs, Devil's Fork, Cat Eye Sink... Take your pick."

"Some of the emails were enigmatic, I was wondering if you would take a look at them for me."

"Is Pete missing again?" she asked sardonically.

"I don't know, I didn't call him. You're much better looking than he is. It was an easy choice."

Her heart skipped and she smiled. "Flattery will get you everywhere, Detective Malone. Where shall we meet?"

Andie called Stacy and asked her to meet her and Sean at the diner near their old high school. The rusty old Chevy that had stayed behind her the whole way from her office sped past as she pulled the Volkswagen into the parking lot. Once the car was turned off, Andie texted Kallie to let her know that she was going to be home late.

"Finish homework before TV. There is cereal and leftovers. No Jordan over."

"Whatev," Kallie replied. Andie couldn't be sure, but she had to assume that meant "I got it Mom, and I will follow your wishes." Somehow she doubted it though.

Chapter Sixteen

Andie was the first one to arrive at the diner. The nostalgic smell of all-day breakfast and coffee greeted her as the bell over the door sounded. The walls were covered in photos of every Pope that had ever lived, some framed, some brown and curling at the edges. There were pictures of Greece everywhere, and in the middle of the wall behind the register, there was an old photo of the original owners of the restaurant.

The image was faded and yellowed. The paper it was printed on had the fuzzy quality of Andie's parents' wedding photos. The two people in the picture had curly hair that stood out like tightly wound, brown cotton balls. The glasses that they both wore were heavy plastic and took up most of their faces. They were posed in front of a marbled blue background and Andie could almost hear the sounds of the Sears photo salon where the picture was taken.

"I remember their funeral," Stacy's voice said at Andie's shoulder.

Andie jumped but then looked back at the fading photo.

"Yeah, that was hard. School was never the same after that."

The mom had worked as the lunch lady at their middle school. A car accident had killed them both when Andie and Stacy had been in seventh grade. Holy Trinity had not been able to accommodate everyone who wanted to attend their funeral mass; the line of mourners had been down the block and around the corner.

"That was sad," Sean said as he came in and saw what they were staring at.

Andie turned around. In spite of her mournful memories, she felt her heart flutter again.

"It was," she said to him.

"Hey buddy, what's up?" a sturdy man came out from the kitchen and embraced Sean. He kissed Stacy and Andie on the cheeks. The apron he was wearing was covered in brown and yellow stains, some faded and some still crusty from the day's cooking. When he was close, Andie could smell the years of grease in his clothes.

Like most of the other Greek establishments around town, when the original owners were not alive any longer, this diner had been taken over by family. The lunch-lady's son was too young at the time of his mother's death, so his uncles had pitched in to keep the place going until this young man could graduate from high school and start running the business.

"Sit wherever you want," he said with a smile. "I'll bring some soup."

They found their way to a well-known booth in the back of the restaurant. The cracked vinyl still cut in to Andie's legs as she slid across the bench seats; she could see where she had tried to tape one corner down years ago.

"The tape's still here," she said to Stacy with a smile.

"Yeah, my initials, too." Stacy traced her fingers over the S.A. that she had gouged into the booth wall. "I don't get out here as much anymore," she said sentimentally.

"Me either," Andie said.

Sean was pulling out a file from a soft brief case he had with him. "I come in for breakfast every Saturday," he said. "Stavros takes a break and sits with me, it's cool."

Andie and Stacy exchanged looks that clearly said, 'I thought we were the only ones with standing Saturday morning breakfast dates.'

"What's this?" Stacy opened up the file Sean had laid on the Formica table. She pulled out the pictures that Andie had seen already. Below these, there were copies of emails and receipts. Some things had been redacted, but Andie could still make out what the images said.

"This is what I wanted help with," Sean replied.

Stacy and Andie took turns looking at the new paperwork. The emails were cryptic. They discussed a dive trip, but contained discussion about lanterns and the phase of the moon, like they were going to be diving at night. Mostly the emails discussed who had what gear and where they were all going to meet.

"This one here," Sean pointed to one page, "shows that the missing diver and the Tampa man, our bombing suspect, were not cave certified. This supports what Pete told us." He looked sidewise at Andie.

"Oh, *thavmasia*! I guess he does have the ability to speak the truth," Andie remarked contemptuously.

"It also sounds like they brought Ross along, the diver who Siegel killed, because of his gear and his money. I don't get the feeling the other guys liked him much," Sean continued.

"Maybe that's why they killed him?" Stacy postulated.

"You don't kill someone just because you don't like them," Andie said with a laugh. Neither Sean nor Stacy shared her amusement. "Do you?" Andie looked from one to the other.

"I'm going to give you your own advice on this one: stick to your day job, doc," Sean said with a smile.

Stacy laughed.

Andie pursed her lips and nodded her head. She had seen a lot in the world--various objects stuck in people's rectum, a cockroach climb out of a woman's underpants, and physical and mental abuse of all types—but she still had a basic naiveté that people were fundamentally good.

Sean continued. "I think that Anthony Siegel killed his dive partner because something happened on the original dive, the mystery trip the four men were planning. I think this whole thing hinges around our missing diver from up north." He paused and took a map out and spread it on the table. "From what we can gather they were planning on sneaking on to private property in order to reach their dive site. We can't be sure where it is exactly, but then I remembered the map at Frankie's store. I was hoping you ladies could help me to remember where the red marks were."

The colorful map of Florida had tentative pencil marks where Sean thought the original red circles and lines had been drawn. They all studied the map, leaning over the crisp paper.

"Oh!" Andie exclaimed excitedly. She sat up straight. "I know. There's a story about an old sink hole on a ranch out that way. Apparently, the owner has never let anyone dive it. It's legend in the cave community. We call it 'Cowboy Sink.' Pete's been after the owner of that cow patch for years to let him go in. The one who gets to map it gets to name it. Basically, the one who succeeds in going in and mapping out the whole cave system gets the title of badass in the Cave Diving Community. It's like bragging rights for life."

"Ok, great. That's a start," Sean said as he leaned back against the sparkly vinyl cushion.

"That would explain why they brought Frankie into the mix. They would have needed an advanced technical diver to help with the exploration," Andie added.

"What about Pete? Do you think they approached him to help?" Stacy asked. Sean and Andie told her about the interview at the store the prior Friday.

"As much as it pains me to say, I don't think he was involved," Andie said. "If he wouldn't even fill their tanks, I doubt they would go back to him for help. I'm sure Frankie would have been more than happy to help though, especially if they said they were diving Cowboy Sink. Throw in some buried treasure and I'm sure he was willing to shut down his store just to go diving. Ok, most divers would gladly shut down their day job to go diving, but you know what I'm saying."

"I get it," Sean said. "If they did go into this particular cave, it's possible that not all of them made it out, and that's where I come in." He gathered up the papers that were strewn across the table but left the map spread open. Andie watched his hands as he worked. The tendons were taut and she could see his muscles contract under his tanned skin. She caught herself thinking what it would feel like to have his hands on her face. She shook herself and turned her attention back to their conversation.

"Do you think you would be able to find exactly where the sink hole is?" Sean asked. He pointed back to the state map. Stavros came by with cups of soup and he had to put them down on top of the blue and green image.

"Thanks man," Sean said.

"Any time, bro," Stavros said with a slap on Sean's shoulder.

Andie looked closer at the center of the state and found the area where she was fairly sure the sink was located. She took Sean's pen and circled it.

"Great, thanks. Look, when we get a warrant to go out to the property, do you want to come? I need a diver to go down and check it out. Didn't you say it would be bragging rights if you got to go in first?"

Andie was surprised. "Me? I don't think I'm the one you want. I haven't been in a cave in years. My gear is old and I would have to do a lot of work to get it cave ready. No, I can't do it. Who do you normally call? Wait, Frankie, right?"

"Or Pete," Sean said. He looked away and scratched the back of his head.

Andie sighed.

"Well, did you call the IUR&R?" she asked.

"You guys should totally eat your soup, it's phenomenal," Stacy said with her mouth half full of rice and celery.

Andie sniffed at the warm cup in front of her. Greek lemon chicken soup was one of her favorites, but she was a bit of a snob. If her mother didn't make it, she rarely ate it.

"Yeah, that's my problem," Sean continued. He leaned back against the cushioned booth wall again and closed his eyes.

"The soup?" Stacy asked.

"The International Underwater Rescue and Reconnaissance Committee," Sean laughed. "I called them but they just keep telling me to call Pete or Frankie. I couldn't reveal too much about an ongoing investigation, so…"

Andie understood the dilemma now.

"Ok, let me see what I can do," she said.

"Thank you," Sean said sincerely. His smile was warm and kind. Andie could not take her eyes away from his face. Stacy caught the exchange and in characteristic fashion ruined the moment.

"You guys want some privacy?" she asked.

"Shut up," Andie said with a slap to her friend's arm.

"Ah, just like high school," Sean commented.

That's what I'm scared of, thought Andie.

Chapter Seventeen

Without any better leads, Sean decided to trust Andie's information and search Cowboy Sink for the missing body. Andie and Stacy drove to the dive site the next weekend. Halloween was quickly approaching, and as they drove through the Florida back roads, Andie could not help but notice the sheer amount of inflatable pumpkins and ghosts undulating in people's front yards. The nylon atrocities floated where they were anchored, inflated by a continuous stream of air. *Their electric bills must be immense*, she thought.

"It looks like Home Depot threw up out here," she commented to Stacy.

Andie watched out of the window as the undergrowth grew thicker the further they drove into the center of the state. Pine trees grew up among scrub trees; standing water dotted the detritus that littered the side of the asphalt roads. The air was heavy with the scent of rotting vegetation, and, as they approached their destination, the smell of manure mingled with the thick aroma of decomposing leaves.

Sean was already there, surrounded by ample police support and crime scene specialists. They were asked for ID when they arrived, but when Stacy used her ME badge the police guarding the road didn't even question Andie.

Sean was directing the melee of officers and civilians that had set up camp around the stagnant pond in the middle of the cow pasture. He was wearing his normal khaki pants, but had forgone his standard button down for a more casual polo shirt. His tan skin shone through the light hair on his arms. Andie felt her stomach do a flip flop as she noticed his muscles flex when he waved to them.

"Damn, he looks good today," Stacy commented. "Look at his ass in those pants…" She tipped her head to the side as if she was trying to admire Sean's backside from all angles.

"Seriously, Stace? You give women a bad name."

Stacy parked the car and turned off the engine, but neither woman got out.

"I'm just saying; look at how hot he is!"

"Oh, I'm looking," Andie said.

"I will never understand how you chose Pete over him. Sean is way better looking than that *malaka* that you married."

"It's not all about looks, Stacy. You're as bad as most of the men out there, hell, you're as bad as Pete."

"*Mazepse ti glossa sou!*" Stacy exclaimed in Greek. "Now who's being fresh?! I have never cheated on anyone."

"You've never been in a committed relationship long enough to have anyone to cheat on."

"And look how happy I am!" Stacy smiled. "I just want you to be happy, *hara mou.*" She reached over and pet Andie's hair. Florida's humidity was rough on Andie's curls, and today she seemed to have lost the constant battle with frizziness.

Sean was approaching the vehicle. The women gathered their things and got out of the small sports car.

"I don't know what you did," Sean said, "But the crowd here is off the charts." He motioned to the throng of civilian divers standing behind police tape near the pine trees that bordered the pasture.

"All I did was put out a message that Cowboy Sink had been accessed," Andie looked over at the throng of on-lookers, "and that the police were looking for someone to go in on a Rescue and Reconnaissance dive. From what I see though, not many of them are actual members of the IUR&R committee." She shielded her eyes with her hands and squinted to look into the crowd. "But there-" she pointed, "those are the two I was telling you about."

She waved for a couple to come through the tape. The policeman guarding the area stopped them until Sean's radio crackled and he approved the male and the female to come on to the scene.

Andie, Stacy, and Sean met the pair halfway to the main activity. After hugs with her friends, Andie facilitated introductions.

"Barb, Henry, this is Detective Sean Malone, he is the man in charge of this investigation." Sean shook their hands. "And this is Dr. Anastasia Antonitis; she is the Medical Examiner for Pasco County. She's the one who did the autopsy on the diver they pulled out of Wild Boar Springs."

"It's so nice to meet you!" Barb greeted Stacy warmly. Her face was ruddy and warm. She grasped Stacy's hand with both of hers and smiled. Henry went in for a hug. He was tall like Stacy, but bald. His scraggly beard fit his boyish face.

As they all made their way back to the tent, Barb put an arm around Andie's shoulder.

"I am so happy you called us," she said. "Thank you for giving us this chance."

Andie's joy at the reunion was apparent. "I thought you guys would be perfect."

"Are you coming in with us?" Henry asked.

"No, no, no," Andie protested. "My gear is not nearly in good enough shape, and it has been too long since I've been underground. I'm going to watch from up here." She pointed to the screen that was sitting on a portable table under the tent that served as the command center. The two divers walked to the makeshift control desk. Tech officers who were seated with headphones around their neck got up to let the two sit down.

"Speaking of watching, we have special dive masks for you, if you think you can use them," Sean said, picking up a piece of headgear that contained a built-in microphone and earpiece. "This way we will be able to communicate with you from up here. Do you think we could mount a camera on this? Or will it be too bulky?"

Henry took the new mask and turned it over in his hands. He put it over his face and then inspected it again.

"I am not going in to a new cave with a piece of gear that I don't know and have never tried, sorry," he said as he handed it back to Sean.

Barb took it and looked it over.

"I mean," she said, "If Andie's ready to come pull one of us out if something goes wrong, I guess I could give it a try, but otherwise I'm not using this thing either." She handed it back to Sean, who looked to Andie for help.

"No problem," Andie said quickly. "I told him you might say that. Just know then that we will only be able to see what you are seeing. We will have no way of verbally communicating."

Henry gave the international sign for o.k.: he held up a hand with his thumb and forefinger linked in a circle, the other fingers splayed upwards.

"Alright then," Sean said with a sigh. He put the mask back into the milk crate where it had been resting. "What we need from you," he continued, "is to search as far as you can safely go. We are looking for a body. We're not sure he's in there, but this is the last place we can track him to, so it's worth a shot."

Andie noticed that he left out the information about the dagger.

"We will be watching in real time," Sean said. He picked up a small bundle of plastic and wires that looked like a mini spacecraft from a 1980's movie. "We will attach this to you, somewhere--wherever you agree will be safest. Andie and I have talked about it and she gave me some ideas, but we were waiting on you before moving forward with the plan."

"Good," Henry said as he took the device and inspected it. "I can mount this on my mask without a problem."

"We can help you get your gear, and then one of our techs will mount the camera for you. When you're ready, Andie will take you down to the water. Do you have any questions?" Sean asked.

"Do you have someone who will be keeping track of the dive with a drawing?" Barb asked. She looked from Sean to Andie. "For mapping purposes. And will we be able to get a copy of the footage after the dive?"

"I'll keep track and make a sketch as you go," Andie said.

"And I'll see what I can do about getting you a copy of the video feed. It might be after the case is over, if that's ok," Sean added.

"Ok with me," Barb said.

"Fine here," Henry added. "Just as long as we get our names on that map, whatever you want is fine." He smiled and patted Andie on her shoulder.

"Do you need help getting your gear?" Andie asked.

Sean facilitated the duo driving their dive truck through the police barrier and on to the field. Stacy took up a position on a folding chair in the grass. She didn't get too close to the water though. As a native Floridian, she was raised to know that you never go near fresh water anywhere in the state until you know what's going on under the surface. Alligators live everywhere.

Barb and Henry were as meticulous as Andie had hoped they would be in preparing their gear. They checked their own, and then checked each other's. They got into their wetsuits as their masks were being fitted with the cameras.

Andie walked Barb and Henry down to the water. Mud squelched and gurgled under her feet as she carefully picked her way across the ground around the pond. She was carrying Henry's side-by-side tanks and his buoyancy control device.

"Hank, this BC is friggin massive! This thing is supposed to hold air, not lead." Andie remarked as she lugged the inflatable vest and large, aluminum air tanks across the meadow.

Weighed down by the tanks and the BC, Andie sank deeper into the boggy grass than she would have if she were on her own. Her footing became more secure as she reached wooden planks placed over the soggy cow path. Once the divers stepped into the dark water, however, the mud swallowed their dive boots up to their ankles.

The actual entrance to the cave was deep below the benign looking round pond. The water was dark and Andie could not see far into the depths, even near the muddy shore. There were reeds growing around the marshy edges, and it was clear that the cows visited only one side of the pool. There was a wide trail through the weeds at that side, and hoof prints could be seen where they had crushed the vegetation. The rest of the shores were thick with native flora and could have been home to any number of creatures.

Barb and Henry put on their fins and then Andie carefully handed Henry his tank. Barb had inflated her BC and it was bobbing expectantly in the middle of the dark water. Once the divers were in and their gear was secure, Andie gave them the "OK" sign. They returned it. Andie walked back to the tent and watched as they did a camera check. She leaned out into the open and gave another OK, and then the divers began their descent.

Chapter Eighteen

Stacy brought her chair within view of the screens. Andie sat with pencil and paper, ready to document anything the divers encountered. What she drew now would help Barb and Henry later as they went through the footage. They would carefully sketch out the cave system and eventually release the drawing to the dive community.

The images on the screen were murky. The water was brown and full of ill-defined sediment. Eventually they reached a barrier, a line in the water column where the current was moving laterally but not vertically, and the water suddenly became clear. Andie saw the slope of the soil and rocks where the ground had collapsed into the hollow tunnels below. The sink was old enough to have gathered some debris, but young enough to have maintained some of the original detritus from the collapse.

Soon Barb and Henry reached the bottom. They slowly spun in a 360 degree turn so that the cameras could capture footage of the entire scene. The current was slow but steady. Water flowed out of one opening in the sink hole and across to another. Small, silty specks of sediment floated past the cameras. The divers moved with careful intention, purposefully ensuring that they did not kick up any more of the fine material that rested on the soft bottom of the sink.

Barb pointed down and bent her head so that the people watching remotely could see the floor of the watery space. Hiding quietly on the soft, grey floor material was a moss-covered cow skull. It was surrounded by the bones of the animal that had fallen to its death when the ground collapsed under it. The image was eerie but peaceful. Andie saw Sean shudder.

"You have no idea what's down there, Sean," she said to him. "It's a whole new world."

"I can imagine though," he responded. "I just hope the next bones we find are those of our missing diver. Not that I'm hoping he's dead, but since finding his burned driver's license, I've kind of given up hope of finding him alive."

The entrance into the cave system was surrounded by fallen stones. Sean settled back in his seat as the divers anchored the end of their line into a boulder outside of the cave mouth. Henry pointed to what was left of another dive anchor in a nearby rock. No line was attached to it, but it proved that someone had been there before them.

One at a time, Barb and Henry slowly entered the dark, jagged opening. They laid their dive line carefully, placing their individual line markers as they went. The progress was slow, but Andie could not have been happier with their painstaking attention to detail. The training to become a cave diver isn't just so that instructors can make money. The reason divers trained so hard, the reason it took months of work and preparation to get this far, was so that divers could come out of caves alive.

The divers moved along steadily, their spools of line unraveling as they went, marking their way back to safety. Eventually, Andie and Sean watched as they emerged from the narrow passage into a cavern. Compared to the small aperture of the approaching conduit, the new room was immense. There were stalagmites and stalactites dotting the uneven floor and ceiling. Some tips had broken off and lay on the sandy floor.

There were multiple exits dotting the rocky cavern walls. The divers communicated via hand signals how they were going to approach it. They carefully laid their line around the room, ensuring that they had line markers near the opening to the passage back out. If they lost their masks, they would need to be able to feel their way back out again. Every dive holds risk, so they had to have contingency plans in case of an emergency.

As Barb and Henry approached the different sized tunnel openings, Sean, Andie, and Stacy saw more signs that they were not the first to see the wonders of this underground room. There were large X's gouged into the rock near all but one of the passageways. This last one was marked with a large circle. Henry pointed into the hole repeatedly.

"That's the one," Andie said. She marked the opening on the sketch in her lap. "That's the way they went."

Sean perked up. "Great!"

Then Henry gave Barb the thumbs-up sign.

"So, they are going that way?" Sean asked.

Andie looked concerned. "No, they're turning around, they need to ascend," she replied.

Andie looked at her watch. They had been down for an hour. As it was, they were looking at a decompression time of about forty minutes before they could surface. Knowing Henry and Barb, Andie was sure that they would make a Safety Stop near the top as well. Henry held up his oxygen monitor to his camera and Andie saw that he had only a little more than fifty percent of his air left. She quickly gathered decompression bottles and hurried to the water's edge. She lowered the canisters to the bottom of the sink, suspended on dive line. She anchored the line to a cinder block that was weighing down the wooden planks of the walkway. Barb and Henry would be fine, she was sure of it, but she wanted them to have extra air in case they needed it on the way up.

When she got back, Sean was seated in his chair with his hands in his hair. He looked dejected.

"But we didn't find anything," he said. Andie pulled up a nearby folding chair and sat so she could see both him and the screen.

"It would've been miraculous if we had," she said. "I can see how someone could easily die in that cave. It's deep and it's complicated. Barb and Henry are being safe. Now that they know the first part of the system they can prepare differently so they can go back in and explore the rest."

Sean rolled his neck to work out some of the fatigue he was feeling. "Ok, you're the boss."

Both Andie and Stacy laughed at this.

"Then you should've heard me when I told you that this operation," she twisted around and indicated the pasture and all of the people in it, "is going to take a while."

They watched as the divers slowly followed their line back to the exit. Barb made it first but paused. She waited for Henry, who swam past her and through the jagged opening to the tunnel.

"What was that about?" Sean asked. "Chivalry?"

"Cave diver rule," Andie answered. "First man in, last man out."

***

As Barb and Henry made their ascent, pausing for their decompression stops, Andie watched them closely. She was monitoring for any sign of distress. Sean walked around talking to people, signing paperwork, and preparing for the next step. Stacy was asleep in her lawn chair.

"When can they go back down?" Sean asked when he returned.

"Tomorrow," Andie said.

Her eyes stayed on the screen that showed Barb's camera. It was trained on Henry who was bobbing peacefully nearby, his hands folded in front of him. His eyes were closed; he could have been sleeping. They had only a few more moments in this decompression stage.

Sean ran his hands through his hair. Andie was coming to enjoy this gesture. It was new to him, not something he did in high school. She smiled as her stomach did another flip.

"What?" he said self-consciously.

"Nothing," she said. "It's just…" she paused so she could choose her words carefully.

"You're hot," Stacy's ever uncouth commentary cut through the sound of frogs and crickets singing in the gathering dusk.

Andie pursed her lips and nodded. "I thought she was asleep."

Sean laughed; he smiled at Andie. This smile Andie remembered. This was the same smile that had drawn her to him as a freshman in high school. His eyes crinkled at the corners. His whole face softened.

It's good that some things don't change, she thought.

Andie looked back to the monitor, and then over to the water. The still surface of the sink was broken only by the bubbles released from the diver's regulators. As they ascended closer to the surface, the water bubbled with more vigor, and soon two heads broke through. Andie jumped up and carefully made her way down the planks to the edge. She helped them pull their gear out and together they all returned to the command tent.

"That was amazing!" Barb said as she dried herself off.

Henry was looking over Andie's sketch. "So where are we staying tonight?" he asked Sean.

"Well…I…" Sean stammered.

"You didn't think that far?" Andie asked incredulously.

"I did," he said defensively. "I mean, I did think about it, in case we had to stay. I only reserved one extra room though. I wasn't sure how many of us there would be."

"That's ok," Stacy interjected. "We can take one, and Andie can stay with Sean in the other."

Andie kicked Stacy's chair.

Barb and Henry laughed.

"It's ok," Barb said. "We brought our camping equipment. Is it ok if we just set up near the tree line?" She pointed towards the far side of the pasture, away from where the vans and cars were parked. The foliage was dense. The trees were a mix of pines, elms, and oaks. From where they stood, Andie could see the thick vines that clung to the branches, creating a web of impenetrable vegetation. "We are going to have to make a fire though," Barb continued.

"I'll help you set up," Andie said. She shot a reproving look at her best friend.

The sun was just finishing its dip below the tree line as they made their way towards the edge of the cow pasture. The air was growing cooler with the dying sunlight. Andie pulled on her sweatshirt. Crickets sang their evening serenade; startled grasshoppers flew high and away as Barb, Henry, and Andie waded through the thicker grass growing close to the edge of the enclosure. Andie was grateful for her long pants.

"This should do, don't you think?" Barb asked. She stopped in an area of matted grass near the fence line.

Barb began setting up the tent as Andie and Henry ventured into the undergrowth of the surrounding forest to find wood for a cooking fire. They walked along the straggling wire fence. The evenly spaced posts were old, and some of them sat at precarious angles, threatening to fall into the vines that lived around them. One of these posts seemed to bend lower than the others, however. It seemed to be driven unnaturally close to the ground.

The two stepped over the low fence at that spot. Andie was busy scouring the ground for wood when Henry tapped her arm. He pointed into the foliage. There appeared to be a small trail. Branches and vines had been cut and broken, and the ground cover was crushed. Andie strained to see into the dense vegetation. She looked behind her at the darkening sky.

"We should wait for morning," she said to Henry. He shrugged and nodded.

They continued to gather wood until they both had their arms full. They returned to the campsite and Andie helped to start their cooking fire before rejoining Stacy and Sean at the police tent.

Chapter Nineteen

"Yee-Haw Junction?" Stacy read off of a sign on the side of the road. "I know we can be hicks down here in Florida, but come on people."

"Maybe the founders had a sense of humor," Andie responded. "It's better than tonoto…thontoto…"

"Thonotosassa?"

"Yeah, that one. I can never say it, but there is great diving out that way."

"But at least Thonotosassa is historic. At least the name makes sense. It comes from the language of the native Indians who originally settled that area. Yee-Haw Junction is just dumb."

"Your mama's dumb," Andie added.

"Your mama's so Greek she shits baklava," Stacy shot back.

"That one's true," Andie said. They both laughed.

There was something that happened when they got together that brought out the kid in both Andie and Stacy. They had grown up together; they even went to the same Sunday school. They attended the same Greek private school for elementary and middle school, and then transferred into Tarpon Springs High to finish High School. After graduation, they even went to the same undergraduate college.

Things changed when Andie married Pete though. It was right before medical school, and that is when she and Stacy grew apart. Andie stayed in the south for her medical school, returning to Florida for residency. Stacy traveled further north to try and get a new start. Her training in Virginia served her well as a Medical Examiner, but she said that the snow made her homicidal, so she had to move back to Florida. It didn't take long for the two friends to pick up where they left off, and Andie was grateful to see that their true friendship never died.

Stacy was driving them to the only motel near the dive site. Sean had reserved them a room at the small establishment. He told them they would know it when they saw a neon sign that read "MOTE" and was larger than the actual building itself.

The gentleman in the front office wore large, scratched glasses that slid down his pasty nose several times as they checked in. He pushed them back up with thick, callused fingers and smiled warmly from under a grey moustache.

"The diner is fixin' to close, so hurry on over if y'all need some food," he informed them.

They thanked him and took the plastic key fob. Stacy had offered to leave a credit card for 'incidentals,' as Clarence, the proprietor of the motel, had called them, but Andie just gave him a twenty, which seemed to suit him just fine.

"Cash is king around here," he said with a wink.

Their room was about what Andie expected. It smelled of old cigarettes and mildew, a common scent in Florida. The polyester bedspread was scratchy against her hands as she put her overnight bag down. Andie heard Stacy try the sink in the bathroom. The spout sputtered a few times before the water ran clear.

"We are going to need some bottled water," Stacy said. She had a look of disgust on her face as she peered into the cracked and rusting shower.

"I'm not sure they have bottled water," Andie called to her.

Stacy came back out to the main room. "Everyone in Florida has bottled water," she said.

They changed and headed out for the diner. Sean was seated in a booth already, and Stacy and Andie slid in across from him. Stacy elbowed Andie, telling her to change sides and go sit next to Sean. Andie elbowed her back, but with more force. She wanted to make sure Stacy got the message once and for all.

"Ow! Dammit, Andie!" Stacy yelped. She grabbed her ribs. "Sean, I want to press charges for assault."

"Then I'm pressing charges for trespassing," Andie retorted. She picked up a cracked plastic menu and pretended to be choosing food.

"Trespassing?" Stacy laughed. "Really?"

"Yes, trespassing--into my life," Andie said, slapping the menu down onto the sticky Formica table. "Get your unnaturally perfect nose out of my business!"

Stacy put her hand to her face and wrinkled her brow. "Hey now, leave the schnoz out of this."

Sean cleared his throat.

"You, too," Andie added moodily. "You stay out of this, too."

"Sure thing. Whatever 'this' is, I'm staying out of it," Sean responded.

The waitress came by and took their drink orders. Colorful fish and snakes covered her arms, cascading down a blue waterfall. Andie couldn't help but think about her liver function as she stared at the artwork.

"Liver failure," Stacy said as the girl walked away.

"That's what I was thinking, unless she has limited her tats to the sleeves, but I somehow doubt it," Andie added.

"Either from congestion or Hep C," Stacy finished.

"Excuse me?" Sean said, looking down the diner aisle to where the waitress was placing their order.

Unfortunately, predicting someone's mode of death was an occupational hazard for Stacy. She could imagine the autopsy, what the organs would look like, and what her findings would be. Andie had the habit of predicting lab results. Either way, it changed how they saw the world.

"I'm not even going to ask any more," Sean said. He raised his hands in the air in surrender. "You docs can be annoying to be around, did you know that?"

"We've heard that once or twice, yeah," Stacy said.

"Look at our waitress's arms when she brings the drinks," Andie said to Sean. "If she gets too many tattoos her skin might not be able to function normally, and her liver can fail. That's what we're talking about."

Sean nodded. "I was actually thinking what a pain in the ass it would be to have to catalogue those if she has ever been arrested."

"See? Every job has its filter through which a person sees the world," Stacy stated.

"So true," Andie said. She picked up the menu again. "Speaking of medical complications from lifestyle choices, my cholesterol cannot handle country fried anything. I guess a feta omelet might work though."

"Don't count on the feta this far outside of Tarpon," Stacy warned.

Andie waited until the waitress had taken their order before telling Sean and Stacy about the fresh 'path' she and Henry found in the woods.

"I figure that maybe we can explore it in the morning? Maybe as Henry and Barb go back into the cave?"

"Don't you need to stay by the monitors and keep sketching their progression?" Sean asked.

Andie frowned. "Right, I forgot about that part." She did not want to miss exploring the woods. The memory of the Spanish dagger taunted her from the back of her mind. Stacy was right, finding hidden Spanish Treasure was every Floridian's dream, even if they were unaware of it. The romance of finding old pirate treasure, or a stash left by conquistadors, was exciting.

She looked to Stacy, who rolled her eyes. "Fine, I will draw while you go into the bug and snake infested Florida wilderness."

"Thank you, Mama," Andie said. She squished Stacy in an awkward sideways hug.

***

Early the next morning, Stacy and Andie drove in tandem with Sean back to the sinkhole. Sean's officers were on site already. Some had never left; they stayed all night to guard the gear and the dive site. The three friends parked and walked to the back of the pasture, where Barb and Henry were making coffee and eating breakfast.

"Good morning!" Barb called as they approached. "It's a beautiful day for a long and dangerous cave exploration."

Stacy sat with the campers as Andie showed Sean the break in the foliage.

"Ok, let's get the dive started, then I will send some officers back there with you," Sean said.

"You're not coming with me?" Andie asked. She was surprised to realize that she had been hoping to share this mystery with him.

He smiled and reached towards her. He touched her face gently; Andie's heart fluttered. "I have to stay near the site in case Barb and Henry find the body."

The excitement of the caress was crushed by the mention of a possible dead body. Andie nodded. "Of course."

When Barb and Henry were ready, they all headed to the command tent. Andie and the divers repeated their steps from the day before. They meticulously checked gear, carried tanks and fins to the water, and then Andie watched them descend. This time, however, they took multiple stage bottles with them. They would have to leave oxygen reserves along the path in order to make it further into the cave system.

Andie waited long enough to watch Barb and Henry make it into the cavern. They tied off their stage bottles, and as they moved into the passage marked with the 'O' she decided it was time to go. She turned and gave Stacy directions to make a good pencil sketch for the divers.

"I know Andie, you have told me three times now," Stacy shooed her away. "Go forage. Just don't get bit by any cottonmouths or anything."

Andie kissed her on the top of her head. "That's what I have armed guards for." She indicated the officers Sean was sending with her into the woods.

Stacy looked up at the officers. Her glance turned into a second look at one of the men, and she looked him up and down. "You any good with that gun, young man?" she said with a half-smile on her face. The young patrolman chuckled uncomfortably. He looked at Sean, who just shrugged and shook his head.

"Say yes," Sean said in a stage whisper. "It's better to just play along." He handed Andie a bulky walkie-talkie. "Keep in touch," he said to her. "Let me know what you find." He moved his attention to the two young officers waiting nearby. "Don't let her get into any trouble. Don't let her talk you into going too far or taking any chances."

They both nodded. "Yes, sir," they replied.

Andie made a tisk sound with her tongue. "I'm not a child," she said.

"I know," Sean replied. "But don't forget that I know you. And I'm in charge, so suck it up."

Stacy's eyebrows shot up and she made the sound of a cat purring. "Well, Mr. Police Officer, you can just stay here and be in charge of me if you want..."

Andie kicked Stacy's chair. "Ok then," she said, and she moved off towards the forest.

Stacy called after her, "Find out if officer Hot Pants is single, okay?" Andie didn't turn around; she simply raised her hand and waved goodbye as she walked towards the woods.

Chapter Twenty

When they reached the damaged fence post, one officer preceded her into the dense undergrowth, and then one came in behind her. The leader had a machete and whacked at tree limbs and bushes in order to make the narrow trail wider. The air was heavy under the protection of the canopy, but the earthy smell was somehow cleaner than in the meadow. The smell of the moist soil permeated every step, and as the officer cut at the wood and leaves, Andie could smell the scent of fresh vegetation.

It wasn't long before Andie saw something red through the vines in front of them. Soon they reached a small clearing. Next to a circle of scorched and cracked rocks, there was a collapsible nylon camping chair. Lying on its side near the chair was an old bucket. A length of white nautical rope was attached to the bucket handle; it lay in a disorganized heap amidst the leaves near the fire circle.

The officers orbited the clearing, looking carefully at the ground and the surrounding foliage. Andie stepped in to inspect the bucket. The most direct route was through the fire circle, so she stepped over the stones. As she stepped inside of the rocks, as she put all of her weight on her front foot, the ground underneath her gave way. Her leg fell through the sticks and leaves. She felt her groin muscles burn as half of her hung into the unknown while the other half lay splayed at an unnatural angle.

She shrieked when she fell, and the officers rushed back to her. They each grabbed one of her upper arms and pulled her out of the hole. Andie massaged her burning inner thigh. She was sure she had torn something, but she was less worried about that then she was intrigued by the hole into which she had fallen.

"Give me one of your lights," she said to the officers. Then she added, "Please."

She shone the heavy MagLite into the darkness. The light, as strong as it was, simply died in the dark of the deep tunnel. Andie got on her hands and knees and stuck her head into the opening. She heard the distant sound of running water; she smelled the distinct sharp odor of sulfur, mixed with the earthy smell of damp moss.

"Hello?" she yelled down. The echo was delayed momentarily, but her voice did come back to her. She turned to the officers, "Call Sean, um, Detective Malone. Tell him what we found."

Andie sat up and reached for the thick nylon rope. She started to lower the bucket into the darkness. Carefully, hand over hand, she lowered the container down the dark burrow. She felt it hit water and she let out more rope. She felt the pail hit the bottom. She looked up at the policemen, startled and excited. They were simply standing nearby, staring at her.

"Didja call him...?" she asked slowly.

Officer Hot Pants fumbled with his radio, "Oh, right."

Gently, Andie began pulling the container back up from underground. Soon she heard Sean's voice come from the machine in the young cop's hand. It was mechanical, distant, and tinny. "Yes? What?! Will someone respond? Is everyone alright?" The man holding the radio backed up and gave Sean an update about what Andie was doing.

"He wants to talk to you," he said, walking back to the crude stone circle. He handed Andie his radio.

"I found a bucket, and then I lowered it into the hole until I felt it hit water," she said into the bulky black machine. "But then you will not believe what was in the bucket when I pulled it back up."

Sean's voice came back, loud and full of static.

"Oh, I'm sure I will believe it. Andie, the divers found some kind of cavern. The water runs through it, but there is a pocket of air, an area where they can emerge. The image coming up from the divers showed a bucket being lowered past them and into the water. They're just coming out of the water now."

Andie shoved the scratched black radio back into the hands of Hot Pants. She got on her hands and knees again and yelled, "Barb? Henry? Can you hear me?"

"Andie? Is that you, baby?" she heard Barb's voice call back.

"Well I'll be damned," Andie said to no one in particular. "Yes, it's me. Holy shit!"

"And sweetie, you will not believe what we found down here."

***

The trip back to the base tent seemed much quicker than the trek out. Granted, Andie all but ran through the woods and across the field, but still, the anticipation of seeing the footage seemed to accelerate time. The pain in her feet even seemed to lessen as she high stepped through the undergrowth and over the grass in the pasture.

She arrived breathless at the tent. One of the monitors showed Henry's live recording of the cavern. The other was being used to review the images from the bottom of the old well. They were rewinding when she arrived.

"Oh my God, Sean, this is amazing," she said. She felt like a child; she felt like all of her daydreams of finding treasure at the bottom of the ocean were culminating in the middle of a manure-filled cow field.

Sean focused on the blurry images that zoomed quickly across the old monitor. Splashes of color flashed momentarily and heightened Andie's excitement. "It is," he said absently. He punched the stop button and stood back.

He crossed his arms across his chest. His brow furrowed; his look far less excited than intense.

Andie watched as the divers glided through the silent calm of the underground tunnel. The section of rock and sand looked like so many other caves in the state. Andie became annoyed, wishing that the video would hurry up and get to the good part. She did not have to wait long.

Soon a faint glow filtered through the darkness. Barb patted Henry and pointed. He gave the OK sign and they swam on, continuing as they went to carefully lay line and place their line markers. As they approached, Andie saw what the color had been.

The tunnel widened like the neck of a bottle, opening into a new cavern. Three tunnels ran from the basin. The first was the one they had emerged from. The second was the source of the light in the room; it led straight up through the ceiling of the small cave. The third appeared to be straight across from them. Sean paused the image and pointed to the screen.

"You see that red?" he asked.

Andie squinted at the mash of grays and blacks.

"That is what I was looking at when you radioed back."

There were spots of bright red that Andie was having trouble putting into context. It was like a Rorschach test: tell me what you see in this mashed up, blurry image? But soon, her mind took in all of the detail; soon she was able to make out the twisted and bloated shape of a dead body.

She covered her mouth with her hand and shook her head. "Is that your diver?"

Sean nodded.

The body was wedged into the third opening of the basin. His face was decaying and bone was visible where his waterlogged flesh was just barely hanging on, floating on the gentle current like a disquieting carnal flag. Andie watched as Henry drifted across the center of the open area. He began carefully searching the body. He pointed to individual images in order to document, pausing to allow for the police to analyze it later. The dead man's regulator, his dive gas analyzer, his gloves… inch-by-inch, Henry examined the body. He was vigilant not to disturb the scene.

Suddenly both divers looked up.

"That must be when I yelled hello," Andie said.

Sean nodded but then pointed back to the image. They watched as a bucket hit the surface and slowly sank through the small underwater room. Barb's camera followed it down, and they watched as it landed gently. A cloud of fine grey material billowed up slowly from where the wood and hammered iron container hit the bottom, and then the bucket fell over.

While the camera lingered on the ground for a mere moment, it was long enough to see something under the silt. Something that was not rock. Andie leaned forward, narrowing her eyes to try and make out what she was seeing.

Suddenly the old white rope holding the bucket went taut again and the pail was lifted back up through the earth. Andie watched as the camera image shifted, emerging from the water, into the small pocket of air. The bucket passed close to the camera and disappeared into the column of light shining down from the surface. The picture on the screen bobbed around nauseatingly.

"This must be when Barb and I spoke," Andie said.

"Just wait," Sean said.

Barb dipped below the water again and the image panned to the floor of the basin. Henry's hand dug slowly into the sediment. As the dark sand and detritus fell away, Andie could clearly see what had been under the silt. Shining up from a gloved hand were five gold coins.

Sean paused the film again. He turned to Andie, his eyebrows raised. Andie looked him straight in the eye. She reached into the pocket of her jeans and pulled out an identical Spanish doubloon.

***

"I wonder if they found the sink or the treasure first," Andie said absently.

She was turning the doubloon over in her hands as Stacy drove them back to Tarpon Springs.

"Weren't you supposed to give that back to the cops?" Stacy asked. She glanced over at the ancient coin in Andie's hand. Andie held it up in the sunlight coming through the windshield.

"I gave Sean the one I showed him; I just didn't tell him I had another one in my pocket. Stacy, you said it: this is lost treasure! Like, real lost treasure! This is history right here." She gazed at the yellow metal in her hand. She studied the profile of the man stamped in the soft material; the words etched hundreds of years ago.

"I bet someone threw this down the well to make a wish," she mused absently.

"Really, Andie? You think that was a wishing well?"

"It obviously was a well of some sort," Andie said. She turned to face Stacy as much as she could in the small space. "It is well known that the Spanish who landed in Florida found the springs; that they used them as sources for freshwater. Why else would there be coins and a dagger in the bottom of that hole? And it didn't seem that it was a sinkhole, the edges were too clean, and it was too straight. I bet someone dug it to try and find water, once upon a time. What if…" Andie looked back out of the window. "What if someone used that dagger to kill someone and then threw it down the well to get rid of the evidence?"

"Oh God, Andie, now who's the one who needs to stop thinking about death."

Chapter Twenty-One

It was hard, after such an adrenaline-filled weekend, to transition back to life as usual. Andie showed Kallie the doubloon, but then locked it in the waterproof safe where she kept important documents. Monday came and went without incident. Sean called and updated her on the excavation of the site.

"You'll get some of the credit, actually," he told her. "As will Barb and Henry, of course." He was busy wrapping things up, but said he would be in touch soon.

Andie smiled as she put the phone down. Kallie was busy working on a project for school, so Andie decided to go to bed early. She sunk quickly into a vivid dream about a deserted island. She was with Sean, who was a merman. She was trying to sell him flood insurance. She was just starting to grow wings and a tail when the Buddhist bells rang in the back of her mind.

She was not sure how long the sound continued before she realized that she was being paged. She patted blindly at her bedside table. Finally, her hand hit the vibrating machine and she stopped the angst producing noise. She could hear Kallie still awake in the living room. Andie sat up and rubbed the sleep out of her eyes.

She dialed the number texted to her by her call service. "This is Dr. Markos, returning a page."

Kallie must have heard her voice because she came down the hall and peeked in through the bedroom door. Andie signaled that she was ok, "Just a page," she whispered to her daughter. Kallie didn't leave.

"No, I heard you," Andie said to her patient. "No, it is ok, don't worry. If your body is following the normal hormonal pattern then you should get your menstrual cycle every twenty eight days...I know...Well, everyone is different, but..." Her patient kept interrupting her. "All I am saying is that it would not be abnormal to get your cycle on the first of the month and then again on the twenty-eighth...is it extra heavy? How many pads are you using in an hour?...ok, that's normal. Are you short of breath, having chest pain, dizziness, extreme cramping?" There was a pause as she listened. She put a hand over her eyes. "I guess I'm confused why you called the on-call service then...ok, I know you got your period sooner than you expected, but other than that has anything else been abnormal about this cycle?...Ok, good. Can you call the office in the morning and talk to Stella? She can get you an appointment to discuss this during regular office hours. Now, if you start having any other symptoms—shortness of breath, dizziness, chest pain—then call back, but otherwise please try to relax and we will see you soon, ok? Good, ok, take care." She hit the end button and threw her phone onto her bed.

"You ok, Mom?" asked Kallie. Andie fell back to her pillows and groaned.

"Yeah, I'm fine, thanks baby."

"Do you need anything?"

Andie rolled to her side and patted the bed next to her. Kallie came in and sat down; she started to tame her mom's disorganized curls. Given her immediate genetics, it was amazing that Kallie was born with blue eyes. The dark hair was expected, but more than once the women at church had whispered behind her back, wondering who the father really was.

"I..." Kallie started. "I don't want you to die," she said finally.

"Oh baby, I'm not going to die!" Andie sat up and pulled her daughter into a hug. Together they leaned against the headboard of Andie's bed.

"But you can't say that, you don't know that," Kallie said. She put her arms around Andie's waist.

Andie moved Kallie back to arm's length. "You're right, I can't say that with one hundred percent certainty. But I can say that if I have any choice, if there's any way, I will *always* come back to you."

Kallie's mouth contracted in a tight-lipped expression of begrudging acceptance.

"Ok," she said. Andie pulled her close again and hugged her tight.

The generic text tone sounded from amidst Andie's quilt, near the end of her bed. She scrambled to find it and when she saw the message, she smiled.

"That red headed guy?" Kallie asked with a knowing look on her face. "I'll let you call him back."

Andie grabbed her daughter's hand as she got off of the bed.

"Kal, are you ok with this? Are you ok with him? I want you to know that no matter what, no one is going to replace your dad."

"Mom, Dad's a douche. I totally want someone to replace him. I'm sick of pretending we're a family, and I want you to be happy."

Andie laughed out loud. "Well, ok then."

Kallie shut the door behind her as she left and Andie settled back against the headboard. She dialed Sean's number. His numbers were in her phone, of course, but he had not quite made it to her Favorites list yet.

"Hey, did I wake you?" he asked.

"No, I got a page first. But I was sleeping before that. Getting blown up, then traipsing through the Florida backwoods finding treasure... it all seems to have put me off of my normal game."

"Andie, being that close to an explosion is not normal. Let yourself rest and recover from it. You'll be ok, just give it time."

She nodded and then remembered he couldn't see her. "Sure, thanks. So, what can I do for you, Detective Malone?"

"Well, I was actually, I'm calling," he stammered. Andie smiled as her heart jumped in an unexpected moment of delight. She didn't rescue him from the awkward pause; she waited for him to pull himself together.

"I was wondering if you'd be willing to go to dinner with me. Like real dinner, not to discuss the case."

"Like a date?"

"Yeah, like a date. Is that ok? I don't want to get in the way if you and Pete-"

Andie interrupted with a snort. "No, there is nothing there with Pete, trust me. And Sean, you have to stop caring what everyone thinks, seriously."

"I have, I mean, I do… I mean," Andie heard him take in a deep breath. "I am better at it when I'm not talking to you."

"I don't know if I should take that as a compliment or not," Andie replied.

"I wasn't joking when I said that it really is you."

Andie smiled and pulled her shoulders up to her ears.

"Dinner would be nice," she said finally.

She could hear the relief in his voice, "Ok, great. Awesome. Friday?"

"Yeah, I have to drop Kallie off at Pete's shop--or try to at least. Do you want to meet at Plaka near the docks, around 6:30?"

"Sounds great," Sean said.

"Ok then, see you there."

There was a pause; neither of them said anything.

"Ok, yeah, so sleep well and I'll see you Friday," he finally said.

"Good night," Andie responded. She ended the call and this time when she threw her phone into her bed covers, it was with the invigorating glee of a first crush.

***

The rest of the week flew by. Andie's run on Friday morning was hot and muggy, but she didn't mind. Her feet were still healing and she should have waited another week, but not running was proving more painful than the cuts on her feet.

Once home from the run, she caught herself singing as she got ready for work. Kallie noticed it too.

"Oh, so you're going to pass me off so you can have your own fun?" Kallie said as they were in the car on the way to school. Andie had double-checked that Kallie's things were packed for the weekend with her father.

"Kallie, I am a grown woman, and there is no 'passing off,' just a regular weekend with your dad," Andie responded in what she thought was her best mommy voice.

"I'm glad you like this guy, Mom," she said. "But don't get crazy and have another baby or something."

"Kaliope Markos! Eww, don't talk about such things."

"Eww? Really? You're a doctor, Mom. Doctors don't say Eww."

"Well, apparently we do." There was silence. "Kallie, are you ok?"

"I'm fine," she said unconvincingly.

Andie pulled up to the high school.

"You don't have to go to your dad's if you don't want to," Andie said softly.

Kallie didn't look up; she kept her gaze glued to the floor of the car.

"Whatever, Mom, it's fine."

"Look, think about it. If you want to stay home, let me know, and I will cancel my date and we will watch a movie together."

Kallie smiled slightly but still didn't look up. "Sure Mom, I'll think about it." She climbed out of the car.

"I love you!" Andie called after her. Her words were cut off by the slamming door.

Dear God, this teenager thing is going to kill me.

***

Maria called a few moments later, as Andie was between the school and her office.

"*Querida, ¿Cómo está?*" Andie answered.

"*Bien, mi amor.* Are you excited about tonight?" Maria asked.

Andie smiled. "Kind of. I just don't want this to be a mistake, you know? He seems to still be, I don't know, the same in some ways."

"Girl, enjoy this. You haven't had any since Pete. Enjoy this. And if we don't see you tomorrow morning, we'll know why."

"*¡Sucio!* No, I'm not sleeping with him tonight," not that Andie hadn't thought about it, but she actually believed in the sanctity of sex, so she wasn't going to start by jumping into bed with Sean.

"Ok, maybe not tonight. Tomorrow night?"

"Maria Consuela Lopez De Castillo, don't rush me!"

Maria laughed. "I'm just saying… come on, I'm married, and I have to enjoy the excitement of something new through my friends. And in all seriousness, *mi amor*, you deserve this. Try not to lose the deliciousness of something new by worrying about propriety."

Andie paused as she pulled into her parking spot behind the office. "Thanks. Hey, I just got to work. I gotta go, but I will indeed see you tomorrow. I love you."

"Love you too, Mama. Have fun tonight!"

Andie turned off the car and gathered her bag. She vaguely saw the old truck drive past but didn't pay much attention. It registered as familiar somehow, but that was a far as her brain went as she walked into work.

Chapter Twenty-Two

Andie left the office without finishing all of her notes. Normally she stayed after closing to finish up her work, but that night she needed to get home and get ready. Kallie was watching TV when she got there.

"I see your bag's by the door, *hara mou*. So, you decided that you do want to go to your dad's for the weekend?" Andie hung her bag on the coat rack and walked in to the living room. She stood in front of the TV, blocking Kallie's view. Kallie rolled her eyes.

"Yes, Mom! Can you move now?"

"Only if there's a please in there somewhere. 'Can you move now, please?' Come on, I know you can do it."

Kallie shook her head and huffed.

"*Please* get out of my way. Happy now?"

Andie walked over and kissed her daughter on the top of her head. "Yes. We'll leave in like twenty minutes."

Andie's choice of outfits was limited by footwear at the moment. The expedition through the forest had slowed the healing process for the wounds on her feet. Running was not helping any, either. The cuts from the muscle shells were healing nicely, but she still had a way to go until she was back to 100%. She knew that there was no way she could pull off wearing heels for any period of time.

Andie quickly showered, and then tried on almost everything she owned. There was a heap of clothes and hangers on her bed when Kallie came in to check on her.

"Mom, it's been half an hour, we have to go," she said. She looked over the mess on Andie's bed and laughed. "Nothing to wear? Feel my pain!"

"Ugh!" Andie exclaimed. "What about this?" she held up a plain black dress in front of her. She figured she could wear flats with it and still look ok.

"It makes you look like you are wearing a black paper bag, but whatever," Kallie responded.

Andie pulled it over her head and slipped on leather flats. She went to her jewelry armoire and pulled out a long string of pearls. She held them up to Kallie, who shook her head.

"You're not going to a funeral, Mom. Look," Kallie walked over and went through Andie's jewelry. "Wear this." She handed Andie a bulky necklace made from pink seashells. "And..." she rifled through the rest of the drawers, "...these." She gave her mother a pair of hibiscus flower earrings.

"Really?" Andie said. "I look like a tacky tourist," she said, looking at herself in her full-length mirror.

"Well, you own them. If they're that awful, why did you ever buy them?"

"Ugh!" Andie groaned, turning around and trying to see herself from behind. "It's October, Kal, this is not appropriate."

Kallie grabbed her mom's shoulders and looked at her seriously. "Mom, just go. I don't think he will care what your jewelry looks like." She spun Andie back around to face the mirror. "You look beautiful, ok?"

Kallie rested her chin on her mother's shoulder and smiled.

Andie reached up and pet the back of Kallie's head.

"Now let's go, before Dad goes poof." Kallie hurried out of the room, and when Andie made it to the front door, she was there with her coat on, holding her bags.

Pete was just locking up when they got to the docks. Andie could see annoyance on his face, but he smiled and gave Kallie a hug.

"See you Sunday?" Andie asked. She was half way turned around, ready to head back to the street when he spoke.

"Sure thing, *manari mou*. Why are you so dressed up, got a hot date?" Pete joked. Andie didn't answer; she just looked back towards downtown. Pete's face hardened. His internal struggle with words was visible, and before he could complete his next thought Andie said, "Sunday, it is then." She kissed Kallie. "Have a great weekend baby; call me if you need me." As Andie walked back to the street, she fought the urge to look over her shoulder. She was sure Pete was still standing where she had left him. Soon she heard Kallie's voice.

"Dad?"

There was a pause and then Pete answered, "Come on *Kallie mou*, let's go get dinner."

Andie crossed the street and climbed the few steps to the long porch that ran along the entire front of one of the local hot spots. The owners of Plaka had moved to Tarpon Springs sixty years earlier, from Athens. They came from a neighborhood near the Acropolis and everywhere guests looked, the decorations reminded them of this fact. They had brought their entire family--children, parents, sisters, and brothers. Now that they were older, their children handled the day-to-day operations. Still, the couple made sure to be there on Friday and Saturday nights.

"Andromeda!" the wife crooned as she saw Andie approach. She grasped Andie's hands and kissed both of her cheeks. "*Ti kanis*. George, *thes pios ine*. Come on, come say hello."

"*Gia sou*," Andie replied with a smile.

The older man shuffled from his seat in the corner of the porch. He kissed Andie as his wife had, and then began talking about his bowel movements.

"*Keereeeae Vasiliki*, is this an emergency right now?" The man shook his head but continued to talk about the quality of his stool. "Ok, then please call the office on Monday and we will make an appointment. Just keep drinking water and eating the prunes your wife stews for you, and we'll figure something out." She patted his hand and then kissed his cheek.

Andie saw Sean at the back of the crowded room. He was seated at a table next to the windows. He stood up when she arrived and then leaned in and kissed her cheek. The smell of him so close triggered a run of palpitations. She had to admit that the chemistry between them was still strong.

Sean pulled out a chair for her and she sat down. She felt his hand brush her arm as he walked back to the other side of the table. Her heart raced.

"Thanks," she said. "Good table choice." She looked out at the marina across the street.

"Thanks. You look beautiful," he commented.

Andie was struggling with how to respond when a young woman in black pants and a white button-down shirt approached the table.

"What are we drinking tonight?" she asked. Her smile was bright and kind.

"I'll have a *Frape*," Andie said.

"I'm good with water, thanks," Sean said.

Andie's feelings of attraction for Sean were wrestling with uncomfortable trepidation. She was always up front with everyone around her; not pulling any punches or sugar coating anything. However, in matters of the heart, this was not always the best strategy. For the first time in as long as she could remember, Andie was at a loss for words.

Dammit! Act normal! she chastised herself.

The waitress returned with their beverages. "Are you ready to order?" she asked.

"Sure," Andie responded, opening her menu.

"Um, I'm not, actually," Sean said.

While he had grown up in Tarpon Springs, Sean was not entrenched in the Greek Community. He ordered his safety option: spanakopita and a Greek salad.

Andie successfully kept the conversation light until the soup arrived. The steaming liquid smelled of fresh parsley and lemon, of chicken and rice. Sean ate the classic Greek chicken soup without a second thought. Andie stirred it around, and then pushed it aside.

"Is everything ok?" Sean asked. He peered into the soup cup.

"Yeah, no, everything's fine. It's just, you know," Andie smiled sheepishly.

"No, I don't think that I know, so please tell me." Sean put down his spoon and returned her smile.

"I'm a snob, alright?" she finally said. "I'm sure the soup is just fine, it's just that... My mom's is better."

Sean laughed. His face shone like a welcoming fire on a rainy night.

It wasn't long before their meals arrived. Sean's flakey spinach pie was artfully cut and arranged with beets and mashed potatoes. Andie reached over and stole a large chunk of fresh feta from the top of his salad. Their eyes met and Sean smiled.

The conversation during dinner did not stray far from small talk, which was fine with Andie. She was not ready to discuss their past relationship or their breakup in high school. At one point, however, Sean asked about Pete. Andie shrugged and pushed the braised lamb around on her plate.

"It's complicated," she said.

"But there is nothing going on there still, right? The last thing I want to do is make life harder for you by interfering." Sean reached out and put a hand over Andie's. His fingers were strong and she watched where the tendons were taut under his skin. Her heart beat hard again and she fought a smile.

"It's not complicated because there's anything romantic still there; it's complicated because of religion and culture. The church does not see us as divorced, and neither does my mother. Some of Kallie's peers, the ones that come from Greek families, have misconceptions about what happens to a kid in a divorced family. It's like she will turn out to be a loose woman, or she won't have good morals because she comes from a fragmented home. It's like because her parents aren't married, she's the one who's broken."

"No offense, but that sounds dumb."

The waitress brought over a plate holding an artistically arranged desert. The baklava had cinnamon honey drizzled over the top; caramelized walnuts lined the edge.

"I didn't order this," Andie said to the waitress.

The young girl smiled and pointed to the hostess stand. The Vasilikis waved happily. Andie smiled warmly and gave a small bow of her head.

"While you're here…" Sean pulled out his wallet and handed the waitress a credit card. George Vasiliki moved with surprising speed through the crowded dining room. He took Sean's card, and the bill, out of her hands. He tore up the check and handed the card back to Sean.

"Your money is no good here, you are no' going to pay. Dr. Markos will never pay to eat here, she eats for free always." He smiled at Andie

"*Keereeae Vasiliki, efharisto, para poli.* Thank you," Andie stood and kissed him on both cheeks.

***

"Is it always like that?" Sean asked later as they strolled down the tree-lined street that ran along the Marina. The air was cooler now and Andie pulled her shawl over her shoulders. She chuckled.

"Pretty much. It's a Greek thing--my patients never let me pay for anything in their places of business. Usually I just leave cash in the plastic containers near the front, for whatever charity they are collecting for at that moment."

"Doesn't that make you feel uncomfortable?"

Andie shrugged. "No, because nothing is ever really free. I get stopped in the grocery store, at the gas station… people ask me about their rashes, their blood pressure, even their poop. It's ok. It's what I do. It's what I love."

Sean smiled. "People just ask me to fix their parking tickets."

"That can come in handy, you know."

His smile widened and his boyish chuckle was an infectious, happy sound.

The air was not humid and the night was pleasant. The relative coolness was refreshing and Andie took a deep breath, thankful for the evening, for her daughter, and her job. The distinctive smell of salty gasoline and decaying marine life filled her nose. The pervasive aroma lay heavy in the cool night air. The quiet sound of boat riggings gently hitting against masts of sailboats felt like a comforting lullaby. These reassuring sounds and smells helped to sooth the nagging anxiety Andie still held in the back of her mind.

Chapter Twenty-Three

They walked in comfortable silence until they came to a small park. There were no playgrounds or jogging paths in this small patch of city land. There were a few benches facing the water; the grass was beautifully manicured, and the palm trees were meticulously trimmed. They only thing that seemed unchecked was a robust bougainvillea. The fuchsia flowers flowed like rebellious children, spilling over the cement wall that held back the marina waters below. Andie knew that the lawn and trees were easily tamed, but that it was safer and easier to leave the beautiful purple-pink bush alone. Just under the brilliant color of the flowers, the plant hid deceptively vigorous thorns.

"Is here ok?" Sean's voice pulled her back to the night air.

"Sorry, yeah, sure."

They sat down on a bench that looked back at the marina. Neither spoke; together, they watched the boats gently bob in the water. From where they sat, Andie could see the burned-out shell of *Fin Fun Charters*. She started to replay the day of the explosion in her mind.

"Have you guys found Frankie yet?" Andie asked.

"Not yet."

She could tell he had been thinking about the same thing. They both continued to stare at the vessels anchored around the open water of the Marina.

"I wonder what he had to do with the divers. He wasn't part of the emails, was he?" Andie asked.

Sean stretched his arm along the back of the bench and turned to face her. He didn't speak right away.

"No," he finally said. "He wasn't. How well did you know him?"

Andie shrugged and gazed past the docks and out into the intercoastal waterway. "I've known him since Pete opened the store ten years ago. He's never come over for dinner or anything, but he was always kind. Even when Pete was being a slime ball, Frankie always treated Kallie and me with respect."

"I have to ask, if Pete was such a slime ball, why did you stay with him for so long?"

"We were talking about Frankie, not Pete," Andie replied. She was not amused with the change of subject. "And I'm not ready to have that conversation with you yet. And while we're talking about conversations I'm not ready for, I also don't want to talk about our break up, so please avoid both subjects for the time being."

Sean lifted his hands in the air. "Ok, ok. That's fine. And I apologize if I overstepped a boundary." He smiled warmly at her. The crinkles at the corners of his eyes were disarming; the blue sparkled in the fluorescent glow of the park lights. Andie's heart jumped again. Sean's face was open, honest. For the second time, she found herself lost for words. It was ok though, because Sean continued. His tone of voice held an attractive authority.

"But just so you know: I saw that writing on the wall in high school. I have worried about you ever since." His charming smile faded and Andie had a glimpse of the flame he had been carrying for her all of these years.

She swallowed hard over unexpected tears. She couldn't speak so she just nodded. "Ok," she finally said. She cleared her throat and drew in a calming breath of the thick, salty sea air. She looked back towards the explosion site again.

She brought the subject back to the investigation. "What did your people find in this marina?"

"What do you mean?" Sean asked.

"On these anchors here," she indicated the water in front of them. "What did the divers find here?"

"We haven't sent anyone into the water here."

"You haven't sent divers into this marina yet?"

He raised his eyebrows. "Is there a reason to? We did check all of the anchors at the other site, but not this one. Is there something you know that I don't?"

"Sean, come on! This is obviously related to diving. What did your divers find when they went into the water at the other place?" She clearly knew the answer already.

"The ID of the missing guy, but-"

"So, wouldn't you think that you might find something else underwater here? Frankie's store was right there." She pointed towards the burned-out building.

"Are you done?" Sean asked. His assertive voice returned and Andie found herself smiling at how attractive it made him. "This isn't some television show, Andie. We can't just send a swat team of divers into the Tarpon Springs Sponge Docks Marina and not expect blow-back from the city, especially without any probable cause. This city survives on tourism, if you haven't forgotten."

Andie was ashamed to realize that she had been speaking as though she was smarter than the police. "Sorry," she said. "My mouth again. It always seems to get me in trouble."

Sean's face shifted, softening as his happiness reached the corners of his eyes. He searched her face. "It's ok. It's one of the things that is so beautiful about you."

"My arrogance?"

"Your mouth."

Andie would have laughed at the pure sophomoric nature of the line, but she was too absorbed with the feeling of his lips on hers.

***

As they walked back along the water to their cars, Andie realized that the stores along this strip of the city were already closed. The night had slipped away; she had not realized how late it was. There were a couple of bars still open. A mediocre acoustic version of a Jimmy Buffet song spilled into the street. The singer's voice tumbled out of the amplifier, muffled, like someone without any knowledge of music equipment had hit the power button and then turned the control knobs randomly. Andie couldn't make out the lyrics.

"What is that song," she stopped and listened. "'Hamburger in Heaven?'" She felt a soft breeze on her face and smelled a mix of suntan lotion and wood floors soaked in beer. Andie remembered why she avoided downtown on weekend nights.

Sean let out a loud laugh. "'Cheeseburger in Paradise.' What kind of Floridian doesn't know 'Cheeseburger in Paradise?' It's as classic as 'Margaritaville!'"

"Hey," she pointed an accusatory finger at him. "You keep your celestial meat sandwiches and I will stay on my own filo and honey covered side of the street."

In one swift movement, Sean scooped Andie into an embrace and entwined his fingers into her hair. He pulled her towards him, hovering above her face for a moment before kissing her again. This time his kiss felt different; this time there was hunger in his movements. He bit gently at her bottom lip and Andie stood on her tiptoes as she pressed herself towards him. She wanted more, she wanted to throw all caution to the wind and bring him to her house.

But she didn't. She reined in her desire and placed her hands on either side of his face, pulling away slightly.

"Thank you for a wonderful evening," she said. "I think the last time I felt like this was, well, when I was a teenager." She kissed him once more on his soft lips. "Will you walk to the end of the dock with me?"

Sean's breath came fast and Andie watched emotions flit across his face. Finally, he responded, "Of course."

His strong fingers cradled her hand as they walked towards the water. He felt protective yet gentle. His touch was warm and soothing. She intertwined her fingers with his and felt his palm against hers. He glanced at her and his smile triggered a now familiar fluttering in her chest.

When they reached the police tape surrounding the site of the explosion, they lingered. As Andie gazed at the damage, she was overcome with gratitude. She thought back to her conversation with Kallie earlier in the week. She hoped she would be able to keep her promise to her daughter.

They walked to the end of the pier and leaned against the railing. The wind was stronger out in the channel, away from shore. Her hair blew out behind her. Tarpon Springs is situated on the Gulf of Mexico, outside of Tampa. It's considered part of 'the greater Tampa Bay area.' Throughout her childhood, Andie had heard stories about The Bay, and how the intercoastal waterways had been used by pirates. Every year there is a celebration of these privateers. It is like a local Mardi Gras, complete with beads and scantily clad women. Andie's mother never let her go, but everyone in the area was a part of the Gasparilla Festival whether they wanted to be or not. The city of Tampa hosts a huge parade. Locals dress up in their best feathered hats, knee-high leather boots, and eye patches. By evening, local emergency rooms are full of drunken party goers, and the whole next week Andie has to deal with flare ups of alcohol-related illnesses.

Even as a child, Andie used to stare out at the water, imaging days gone past, when Tall Ships dominated the seas. She would watch the movement of the water for hours, lost happily in imaginings of pirates and mermaids. As a diver, she had been in the channel waters before, and while there wasn't much to see under the water, the romance of those days continued to intrigue her.

She was enjoying the wind on her face, and was just considering another kiss with Sean when she saw movement on the dark, gentle waves. She squinted and in the low light, she could just make out a small craft at the mouth of the marina. She tapped Sean and pointed it out.

Together they strained to see if they could make out any details.

Why would a small craft be out in the middle of the night?

As if reading her mind Sean said, "There's only one reason for someone to be out in a skiff with no lights at this time of night."

They moved quickly back to the road in front of the restaurant where they had eaten dinner. Sean opened the trunk of his car and pulled out binoculars.

"You keep binoculars in your trunk?" Andie asked. Sean put them to his eyes and scanned the marina for the small boat.

"I'm a cop, Andie," he said without looking away from the boats. "Ok, I see them."

"Them?" Andie asked. She stood up on her tiptoes and leaned in to him, like somehow, she would be able to see what he was seeing by being closer to him. He turned his head and looked down at her face near his shoulder. He smiled.

"I like having you this close to me," he said.

Andie reflexively backed down.

"Sorry," she apologized.

"For what? Did you not just hear me say I liked having you so close to me?"

"For crowding you, I mean, while you're trying to investigate suspicious behavior."

Sean laughed again and looked back to the water. He handed the binoculars to Andie and helped her find the location where the craft was now tied up to a sailboat.

"Keep an eye on them; I'm going to call for backup."

Andie watched the two men who were dressed in dry suits. The heavy one turned to pick something up and Andie exclaimed, "It's Frankie." She looked closer and she recognized the other diver as her mystery near-drowning victim.

"It's Frankie," she said to Sean when he returned.

"I saw that," he commented as he took the binoculars back. "Look, Andie, this has become a situation. I have to do this, like I have to officially go on duty." He glanced down at her. His eyes were apologetic. "I had hoped to drive you home, but I can't leave now. Can I call you tomorrow?"

Andie jutted out a hip and crossed her arms. "Are you sending me home?"

He touched her face. "I am," he said firmly.

Andie backed away and opened her mouth in protest. At least five retorts formed in her mind but she didn't say any of them. She simply snatched her bag from the ground dramatically. The behavior reminded her of Kallie.

That apple really did not fall too far from this tree, she thought as she stalked back to her car and drove home in a disappointed huff.

Chapter Twenty-Four

Andie listened to angstful female folk singers the whole way home. 'I went all the way to Paris, to forget your face…' She humored her childish feeling of rejection. But her indulgent self-pity was interrupted as she closed and locked the front door of her house. She heard the unmistakable sound of her child crying. She quickly hung her bag on the coat rack and kicked off her flats.

"Don't eat those," she said sternly to Athena before hurrying up the stairs towards Kallie's room.

Years ago, when she bought the house, Andie had paid to have the attic refinished before they moved in. The builders had created an air-conditioned storage area, which was priceless in the Florida humidity, but they also had artfully built a bedroom for Kallie. She had been verging on her teen years and Andie knew that she could use privacy. The sloped ceiling gave the space a cozy feeling, and the window extended into a dormer. There was a seat built into the recess where Kallie spent hours reading, and writing dramatic teenage poetry about love and heartbreak.

Andie knocked on the door before she pushed it open.

"*Kore mou*, what happened? Why are you home? Did your dad do something? I'll kill him if he did." She sat on the side of the bed. "Oh, honey, are you ok?" Kallie was hugging a pillow to her chest, her knees drawn up. Her face was red and puffy. Andie reached up and wiped tears away from her cheeks.

"I hate everyone."

Andie did not immediately respond. She moved next to her daughter and smoothed her thick hair away from her face.

"Is there a particular someone who triggered this?" she asked.

Kallie didn't answer. Instead she fell, face first on to her bedspread. Her shoulders shook with a new wave of sobs.

"Ah," Andie said. "Jordan?" Kallie nodded, still face planted against the bed.

Andie laid herself over her daughter and hugged her. The only sound was Kallie's crying. Finally, Kallie wiped her eyes and nose on the hand quilted fabric and sat up.

"He's taking Brianna to the formal," she said through hiccoughing breaths. "And now I have this dress, and..." She broke down again, sobbing into her pillow.

Again, Andie reached to her daughter to pet her soft hair. She looked at the pain on Kallie's face and her heart broke.

"Brianna sucks," Andie said finally. "And Jordan has got to be the stupidest guy in all of Florida. He obviously doesn't know what a gem he had." She pulled Kallie into a hug. "And go ahead, snot all over my shoulder. It's been a few years since you used me as a tissue and I was starting to miss it."

Kallie released an involuntary laugh.

"Look, I know I'm supposed to be a good mom by telling you that it'll all be ok, that this will pass, you're young, that you'll find someone else, et cetera; that you have to learn these hard life lessons, that life isn't fair but we have to grow and accept painful situations, blah blah blah. Those things are all true, but heartbreak sucks. It hurts, and it just plain sucks."

"I just don't understand," Kallie said tearfully. "What's wrong with me?"

Andie cut her off, "Listen to me Kaliope, there is NOTHING wrong with you. Unfortunately, it's a normal reaction for you to think like that, but please hear me when I tell you: this isn't about you. This is obviously about him."

"But if I were-"

Andie cut her off again. "If you were what? Smarter, prettier, thinner? Whiter? Blonder, shorter, taller? Sweetie, for whatever reason, this dumb boy had other plans. He made a decision based on something, something that he likely isn't even aware of, and that decision didn't coincide with your plans, and that sucks."

"Are you trying to tell me I'm upset because I didn't get my way? Mom, that's so mean!" Kallie sat against the headboard of her bed and crossed her arms. She drew her knees up to her chest again; her face set into a scowl.

Andie sighed. She knew that nothing she said would soothe the pain of Kallie losing her first real boyfriend.

"I'm saying that as a strong woman, as a smart, capable, strong-willed young woman, you have big ideas about what you want out of life. And I could tell you that all of those dreams will come true, if you work hard, but here's what I've learned to be true: we tend to think that because something makes us happy it therefore is the 'right' thing for us. But sometimes life has other plans. Sometimes we don't always know what's good for us." Andie thought back to her reaction when Sean sent her home and internally rolled her eyes at herself.

"Like Dad?" Kallie looked up.

Andie laughed sardonically, "Yeah, just like your dad. He was handsome, charming, but most importantly: he was Greek. I was so focused on marrying the right Greek man that I ignored obvious signs, that he wouldn't make a good husband. I was driven to have it all; to have a career, a family, and the perfect marriage."

Kallie's tears stopped; she seemed to be listening. Andie tried not to lose steam. "So, I had to give up my idea of what I thought my life should look like. I had to stay in my today, to be grateful for the life I did have, instead of always bemoaning the things that I didn't have."

Andie moved next to her daughter again. "*Hara mou,*" she continued, "I will never regret my time with your father, because I got you. You are the number one best thing that I have ever done, hands down."

Kallie leaned her head against Andie's shoulder. They sat together silently. Eventually Kallie said, "How was your date with the police guy?"

Andie laughed. "It was fine, thank you."

"Did he kiss you?"

"Kaliope! That is none of your business!"

Kallie started to cry again. "Why are boys so dumb?" she asked.

"I don't know honey." Andie hugged her daughter's head where it lay against her shoulder. "I just do not know."

***

Monday morning, Andie put on her running shoes and attempted another trot down the Pinellas Trail. After a few steps however, she gave up and settled for a brisk walk. *Maybe I started back too soon,* she thought to herself.

Her frustration at her body for not instantly healing the wounds on her feet was mounting. She survived a brief internal battle where her brain told her heart that it was only logical that she needed time to heal, and that she should take the advice she gave all of her patients and take it easy.

"Like hell I will," she said aloud. Her voice disturbed birds roosting in the nearby mangroves. With a rhythmic whoosh, they all took to the sky with reproachful squawks.

Sean had called Saturday, but Andie petulantly did not return his call. She blamed it on being childish, but she knew that really, she was afraid of the feelings she was having for him. He called again on Sunday night and left a long message. Andie waited until she went to bed to listen to it and regretted not answering his call.

Now, on the morning of a new week, she was trying to block him out her thoughts. She started to run again, ignoring the pain in her feet. She turned her music up louder than normal as she pushed her muscles to their limit. She was trying to get to the point where all she cared about was breathing. No matter how winded she felt, however, she couldn't help but think about Friday night.

The text tone rang loudly in her ears, interrupting the Metallica she had chosen for the morning's exercise. She let out a quick screech as she tore the ear buds out.

The text was from Sean.

"We need to talk. It's about the case. Call me later."

She started typing three times, and erased each one. She decided the response could wait until she got home. She put her earbuds back in and turned around to head home.

Chapter Twenty-Five

Andie called Sean on the way to work. She figured she would only have a small window of time to talk, so they couldn't get too far into a conversation. She called his work phone number.

"Andie?"

"Yeah, hey."

"Hi. Why are you calling my work number?"

"You said it was case related," she answered. She was turning out of the high school after dropping Kallie off. The traffic was distracting her, and he must have heard it in her voice.

"Is this a bad time? We can talk later if you need."

"No, it's ok. I'm on my way to work though, so I don't have much time."

God, I'm totally being a bitch, she thought to herself.

"Sorry," she said in a softer voice. "I just dropped Kallie off and the traffic is heavy. But don't worry, Mr. Policeman, I'm on Bluetooth, so no driving while holding my phone."

"It's still dangerous and distracting," Sean said.

"Well, take it or leave it, big man," she said.

Sean laughed.

"Ok, ok. Glad to see you are back to your old self again."

There was a pause.

"Andie, look the divers found another lock box. And I can't find Pete, again. He didn't show up at the boat house this morning."

"I'm not his keeper," Andie retorted.

"I can't do this with you right now," Sean said. "I will be at your house after work."

She decided to call Stacy quickly before she made it to work.

"Hey babe, have you talked to him yet?" Stacy said.

Andie heard the bone saw in the background.

"Yeah, I just did, but not about Friday night."

The saw stopped and Stacy's voice sounded closer. "Look Andie, you gotta talk to the guy. Don't be That Girl."

"I will, I promise. I mean, I'm not 'that girl,' I'm just... annoyed at having feelings."

Stacy laughed as the saw screeched to life again.

"But look, I'm almost to work," Andie continued. "Can you come by my house after you get out of work tonight?"

"Sure thing. Is everything ok?"

"Sean said he is coming by and I want you there, too," Andie said as she pulled into her parking lot.

"Dear God, Andie, what are we, twelve? You want me to write the note for you, too? 'Check this box if you like her.'"

"Yes, do that. But try not to get any blood on it, ok?"

Stacy laughed. "I'll see you after work."

Andie threw her phone into her bag and rushed inside.

As Dr. Markos went into the back door of her office, an old pickup truck pulled out from behind a nearby building. It drove slowly past the office and then out on to the road.

***

Stacy pulled up behind Andie as she drove into her driveway. The friends embraced as they both reached the front porch. They went inside and Andie hung up her bag. She changed into her pajamas and got them each a glass of water.

Stacy was standing near the front double windows. She was leaning against the wall, peering into the front yard.

"Andie, have you noticed that truck there?" She pointed to the rusty old Chevy. It was just barely visible behind the neighbor's overgrown shefflera.

Andie peeked through the slotted wood window treatment. "Actually, now that I see it here, I think that I noticed it earlier, at work." She closed the blinds quickly. She rushed to the front door and stood on her tiptoes to look out of the small windows along the top. Only the truck's rusty front bumper was visible from this angle. Andie turned the deadlock. The hard 'clunk' of the brass deadbolt was comforting, but still did not quiet Andie's discomfort.

She heard the sound of a car pulling into the driveway and moved back to the living room.

"Don't worry," Stacy said. She had pulled the blinds back a small amount and was watching the street. "It's Sean." A door slammed and Andie looked through the blinds as well.

"He looks hot," Stacy said. "If you don't want him, can I have him?"

Andie glared at her best friend.

"What?! You're just being a pussy. You need to jump on that hot piece."

"I hate that word, Stacy. And seriously? You're such a freaking hound dog." Andie walked to the front door and opened the deadlock.

Stacy maintained her surveillance of the street.

"Quick, the truck is leaving, make sure Sean sees it," Stacy said urgently.

Andie pulled open the door. Sean was standing there with his hand raised, ready to knock.

"Well, hi," he said.

"Look," Andie said quickly. She pushed his shoulder to turn him around. The tail of the rusty truck was just turning the corner.

"What?" he said, looking back at her.

"That truck," Andie said. She eyed the place where the vehicle had disappeared from view. "I think I saw it at work, and Stacy said it was here when we arrived."

Sean spun back around. "Did you get the plate number?"

"KX7 something something."

"Something something?" Sean asked doubtfully.

"Sorry, alright? I got the first three digits at least, ok?"

She backed away from the door and invited him in.

"Shit, Andie, this is no joke." Sean's face was serious when they reached the living room.

"I'm sorry, ok? I know it's not a joke; I'm a little freaked out, ok? I did my best!" She walked to the leather couch and curled up next to Athena. She pulled a blanket up to her chin. The dog stretched lazily and then reached over and licked Andie's hand with her enormous tongue.

"Big help you were," Andie said.

***

Andie woke up the next morning with a sense of unease. At first, she chalked it up to the fact that it was Halloween, but still something nagged at her gut. In spite of her fear, she tried again to run. Her feet started to throb after only a few hundred yards. Again, she had to be content with a brisk walk.

The trail was misty but cool. Andie was feeling drained from the night before. Sean had stayed to make sure that the truck did not come back. When Stacy left, she made a wisecrack about not getting into any trouble. Andie had not been in the mood.

She also had not been in the mood to discuss her feelings with Sean. He seemed to understand however, and their conversation stayed light until she made him leave.

"Are you sure you want me to go?" he had said at the door. The night had been cool, and they were on their way to a new moon, so it was dark outside.

She had placed a hand on his firm chest. "In all honesty, I would love for you to stay."

Sean's face lit up.

"But I need for you to go. I will call you if I need you." She stretched up to meet his lips as he bent towards her. His kiss had been firmer than the prior Friday night. His body pressed against hers and her resolve to make him leave began to falter.

"No, really," she said, pulling away, "you need to go home."

She was remembering the kiss fondly as she passed a dense stand of mangroves. Something about the thick leaves and the brackish water made her decide that it was time to turn around. As she did, she got the feeling she was being watched. In spite of the pain in her feet, she started running.

She tried to convince herself that she was being paranoid.

Too much of my mother's constant fear of people, she thought to herself.

With every step, the feeling grew stronger. She stopped to tie her shoes, trying not to break into a sprint all the way home. As she squatted close to the asphalt, she looked deeply into the murky foliage. Her imagination was bounding, and she started to freak out as she saw danger in every shifting leaf. She sprinted home and locked the sliding door behind her.

Athena leaned heavily against Andie's legs as she looked out of the glass. The sun was barely up, so the misty dawn laid over the back yard expectantly, like it was at peace with whatever the day would bring.

"You ok, Mom?" Kallie said from the table. Andie jumped.

"Yeah, I'm fine baby. I'm gonna shower, please get ready--we're leaving in thirty minutes." She moved towards the bathroom, stopping to grab a glass of water.

"Seriously, Mom? That's it? No comment about my attitude, no snarky quip about my age or hormones? You must really be upset," Kallie said. She took another mouthful of cereal and put her ear buds back in.

Andie smiled in spite of her nagging apprehension. Still, she checked all of the locks in the house and commanded Athena to stay with Kallie just in case.

***

Andie was jumpy all day. She ordered lunch in for the staff so she wouldn't be alone, and she called Stacy to sit with her as she gave out candy to trick-or-treaters that night. She had just gotten home when Kallie came bounding through the front door.

"You'll never guess who called me after school?" Her face was lighter than it had been since the incident with Jordan and Andie could not help but smile.

"Who?" she asked.

Kallie threw her backpack onto the couch, narrowly missing Athena. "Do you remember that guy from the dock, Damian?"

"Really? The hot EMT? But wait, he's too old for you, Kal!"

Kallie rolled her eyes and sighed. "God, Mom, can you be normal for a minute? Can you just be happy for me? You started it. You're the one who was playing Stella Match Maker."

Andie frowned. She was caught in her own consequences. "Right, ok. So, he called, yay! He was hot. And smart too. What did he say? When is he coming to church to meet Yaya?"

"I asked you to try and be normal, Mom, not obnoxiously Greek, ok?"

"Sorry, I will try. It's just so hard! Years of guilt and indoctrination do not disappear overnight, you know." Andie smiled.

"Anyway," Kallie continued, "He asked if I would go to dinner with him tonight!" she squealed.

"Did you just squeal?" Andie pointed at her daughter. "Like honest to goodness, like a little mouse?"

Kallie tisked at her mother and playfully slapped her arm.

Andie smiled and hugged her.

"Oh baby, I'm so happy for you. And he is half Greek, so at least there's that. But babe, it's Halloween. Aren't you going trick or treating with Shana and Samantha?"

"Well, I called them already, and they say they'll save me candy. They say that I shouldn't pass up a date with a college guy."

This triggered a whole new wave of parental fear in Andie. "Where are you going? You know if you go to the docks, someone will see you and it will get back to your father and grandmother. And don't go anywhere near the Manos Diner, Stavros will tell Yaya at church. What are you going to wear? When is he coming over?" Andie stood up and headed to the stairs, ready to help her daughter get ready for her date with Damian. But Kallie didn't move.

"I didn't say yes, Mom. I told him I had to check with you first," she said.

"Awww," Andie cupped her hands over her heart and moved back to the couch. She put her arms around her daughter. "That is so sweet. And oddly respectful. But I'll take it. I tell you what, call him back and tell him that if he comes over here so I can meet him, and he gives me his cell phone number so I can track you guys, then it's fine. Oh, and tell him he should be prepared to give me his agenda for the night. I want to know where you will be every step of the way."

"God, Mom, do you want a urine sample too? Maybe take some blood, do a background check?!"

"Good idea! Yeah, get his social security number so I can have Sean run his history. And the urine will be good for a drug screen."

Kallie was taking the stairs two at a time. She had almost disappeared into the top floor of the house when she yelled back, "You are so annoying!"

***

The house was quiet after Kallie left. Damian had been a perfect gentleman. He had a detailed agenda, complete with seafood at Cabanas and then ice cream a Strunk's, a locally owned and operated ice cream parlor. He assured Andie he would have Kallie home by ten thirty.

Stacy called and said she wasn't coming over. Apparently one of the new techs at the ME's office was attractive and had invited her to a Halloween party.

"I'm going as a butcher, you know, of humans, get it?" she had told Andie.

Andie relayed her routine warnings: be safe, use a condom, don't go to his house--he could be an ax murderer. Stacy responded in her normal way as well: Sure thing, honey, I'll call you to let you know I'm home safe.

Andie turned on a movie and finished up some patient notes while she answered the door for trick-or-treaters. The candy was gone soon, and she turned off the porch light to discourage any more small ghosts or goblins from ringing her bell. She gathered a good book and grabbed a glass of ice water before she headed into a hot bath. It was early still when she got out. She felt old turning in so early on a Halloween night, but she reflected on how nice it was to get into bed before eleven pm.

She made a cup of tea and was heading to her bedroom when Athena started to bark. The dog was lying on the couch. Her head was lifted, her ears were raised, and she was barking into the air. At first Andie thought it was just more costumed little people coming up the walk, but this was a different kind of bark; this was a different kind of warning. Andie froze. She grabbed her phone and dialed Sean. It rang, but then went to voicemail.

Dammit, she cursed to herself.

Andie called Athena to her and checked the locks around the house. She considered getting dressed and leaving; going to find Sean in person. She dialed his number again as she walked into her bedroom. The giant dog jumped on to the bed as Andie locked the bedroom door behind her.

All Andie had time to hear was Athena's deep growl before she felt the sharp pain in her head, and then everything was dark.

Chapter Twenty-Six

Before she could focus her eyes fully Andie felt the movement of the water all around her. Her nose was assaulted by the smell of fish, gasoline, and mildew. Her entire head throbbed like it was split open. The pain, plus the smell, quickly got to her and she vomited. She tried to move but found that her hands were tied behind her back. She tried to kick her legs out and discovered that her feet were bound at the ankles. Close by, she heard the smack of water against the fiberglass where her head was resting.

A small amount of light filtered down narrow stairs from above. It was the yellow of old fluorescent light and Andie could not help but remember the day they found her patient dead in his home. Her head pounded, and as the boat rocked, she heaved again, the acidic odor of her vomit mingled sickeningly with the stench of her new surroundings.

As her eyes adjusted, Andie saw that the boat she was in was old. There were rusty puddles of water sloshing around the small space. There were rotting piles of anchor line, and old life jackets covered in mildew, discarded and decaying. There was the vague outline of something large and solid nearby, but the edges weren't defined and Andie couldn't make out any details.

She scooted around, looking for something sharp so that she could cut herself free. Her shoulders slid against her vomit on the peeling fiberglass walls of the room. Every time she moved, her head pounded and a new wave of nausea hit her. She slid down and fell against the solid object next to her.

Suddenly, footsteps sounded on the deck of the boat. Andie went limp and closed her eyes. What light shined through her eyelids was blocked out for a moment, but then returned. She heard the sound of a boat engine trying to start. The old Evinrude sputtered but didn't catch. She smelled the spent gas vapor. The engine turned over again and her head swam with the overwhelming odor of fuel and vomit and she wretched, again. This time the engine started. It idled weakly but soon died. Footsteps headed to the back of the boat and she heard the engine cover open.

Andie used the moment to pull herself over the solid object that shared the wretched space with her. She pushed her feet against the vomit covered hull. She edged her arms around as best as she could to try and get a hold of anything she might be able to use to get herself free. Her hands grasped at the hulking object next to her, and she felt the unmistakable feeling of flesh. Cold, dead, flesh.

Her heart pounded in her throat. She tried not to scream. With a final push against the slippery wall, she fell backwards over the dead body. She hit her head on the bottom stair and vomited again. She had to turn her head quickly to let the vomit leak down her cheek. She paused and strained her ears. She could still hear the sound of mechanical tinkering where her captor was trying to fix the engine.

She moved herself around so she could see the face of the corpse she was laying against. The round, obese face was familiar, even in death.

God, Frankie. She whispered a quick prayer in Greek.

The sound of the engine cover dropping back into place made Andie freeze and close her eyes. Footsteps quickly made their way back to the console. The engine turned over again and this time it roared vigorously to life. She heard heavy lines falling onto the deck, as the boat was untied from the dock. Soon they lurched backwards. The engine sputtered again and threatened to stall. A man's voice swore.

But the engine continued to run, and soon they started moving forward. The waves were choppy and Andie fought against her pounding headache and nausea. Her mouth was dry with the acid from her vomit; she could taste the bitterness all the way into the back of her throat. She felt herself bounce against the wall and Frankie. Then finally, with one particularly violent roll to the side, Andie felt her shoulder hit something metal.

It took her a few tries but soon she got her wrists situated over the forgotten, rusty anchor that was lodged, broken, under the stairs. She sawed at the ropes that held her wrists tightly. Her skin was raw where the rope cut into her; the muscles in her shoulders began to burn with the unnatural position and effort it was taking to cut the bindings.

Finally, Andie pulled her wrists free and she almost screamed as her hand smacked against the bottom of the stairs when it flew free of its ties. She quickly climbed back over Frankie's body, out of the small rectangle of light that bounced nauseatingly with the movement of the craft. She reached down and started to undo her ankles. Now that she could see better in the darkness, she noted that what she thought was rust in the mucky water at the bottom of the hull was not simply the remnants of corrosion. Slimy whirls of blood swirled in the decaying liquid. The movement of the boat churned the water into an unnatural soup of live cells and rust. Andie reached up and felt the back of her head. Her hair was matted and sticky.

She was staring at her blood on her hand when the engine sputtered and died again. The male voice uttered a loud expletive and ran to the back of the boat. Andie thought this might be her only opportunity. She felt around for anything she could find. She had to reach into the dark water that sloshed wildly with every wave. She felt the sick rise in her throat again, this time it splashed into the bloody puddle. The mix of vomit, rust, and blood splattered onto her arms.

Finally, her hand closed around something solid. She pulled it out and saw that it was an old nautical wrench. She climbed the ladder slowly and carefully peered over the top rung. The skinny man she had rescued was bent over the old engine. Andie tried to keep herself as small as possible for as long as she could, but then finally, after a plea to God for help and protection, she ran full bore out of the hull, directly towards her captor.

Chapter Twenty-Seven

She brought the wrench down hard against his temple. She was aiming for a soft spot, to try and do as much damage as possible, but she missed and hit him right above his ear. He screamed and grabbed his head. It took him a moment to realize what was going on, and in that time, Andie had made it back to the console. She jabbed at the emergency signal. Nothing happened.

"Are you kidding me??" she screamed.

The skinny man slammed into her from behind. He encircled her with his strong arms and attempted to lift her off of her feet. Andie dropped her center of gravity, trying to make herself as heavy as possible. The boat listed violently. The man lost his footing and he and Andie toppled into the captain's chair. Andie pulled herself away from him and ran to the end of the boat, ready to dive off into the marina.

As she ran, she saw the light of the docks in the distance. The motor had stalled at the mouth to the cove. Suddenly, one of her legs was pulled out from under her and she fell hard on to her chin. She felt shooting pain in her head as her teeth jarred together. She tasted blood in her mouth. The strong hand that held her quickly pulled its owner on top of her. He grabbed her wrists and then hit her across the face. In retaliation, Andie brought her knee up between his legs with as much force as she could muster. She was gratified by his howl of pain. He released her hands as he fell to his side.

Andie stumbled to her feet. Blood was flowing from her mouth and she tried not to wretch as she swallowed the warm, metallic tasting liquid. The pain in her head was worsening, which she did not think was possible, and it made her dizzy. The waves were choppier and, as a particularly tall crest hit the side of the boat, the decrepit craft began to rock wildly.

Andie moved towards the old motor, towards the end of the deck and freedom. She was still convinced that she could make it back to shore safely, but soon her attacker was on her again. He grabbed her shoulders and jerked her backwards. The movement of the boat caused them both to stumble, and Andie caught herself on a piece of PVC pipe meant to hold fishing rods. She put a foot up on the railing and leaned forward to dive over the side. The Skinny Man came up quick behind her. He put his elbow around her neck and squeezed. Andie thrashed violently and, as the boat pitched to the side, they both toppled over the rail, into the cold, October water.

As Andie hit the water, the air was knocked out of her lungs. The man released his grip when they hit, and Andie pawed her way desperately to the surface before she had to draw another breath. Her head broke through and she gasped, pulling in a lungful of cool air. She quickly spat out a mouthful of bloody salt water.

She looked around and found the light of the shore. Andie swam towards safety as quickly as her beaten body would let her. While she concentrated on breathing, the part of her mind that was in full panic mode was not surprised when she felt someone grab her legs. He pulled her under and the salt water stung her head wound. She twisted her body and reached towards him. She grasped at him like a trapped cat, trying to find something to claw, something to rip at, something that would free her from his deadly grasp.

As he pulled himself up her body, he dragged her further down. Soon they were face to face. Andie couldn't see anything in the murky water; her eyes burned as she tried desperately to see through the salt and silt. She tasted the spilled gas. It choked her; it burned the raw flesh in the back of her throat, and seared her esophagus as it reached her stomach.

I should never have saved you, you son of a bitch, she thought. *I need a soft spot, which soft spot...* She quickly reviewed her knowledge of anatomy.

She was desperate to live, desperate to see Kallie in the beautiful dress hanging in her room. She reached forward and got her thumbs into the inner corners of his eyes. She dug her fingers in, angling her joint so that her nail pierced the tissue and penetrated the orbital cavity. The man released his hold on her and Andie felt her thumbs hit the back of his eye sockets. She quickly tightened her hands into fists and pulled them firmly towards her. Now free of his grasp, she felt his eyes in her clenched fingers. Her throat was on fire as she wretched, again. She opened her hands and released the firm, fleshy, dismembered orbs into the dirty water.

She felt her captor flailing nearby. She kicked out at him to push him away, but her feet hit something infinitely more solid, infinitely more terrifying. She realized that it was not only the skinny man flailing around that she felt. The movements were strong and formidable. A bull shark had followed the scent of their blood and was circling where they struggled.

It took everything she had to not freeze in panic. She surfaced again and started to cough. Soon, she was able to draw in a piercing breath of cold air. Her heart thundered in her chest; she felt like she was going to lose bladder control and vomit. She looked towards shore but felt the fear of never seeing Kallie again as she thought of having to make it that far while there was a bloodthirsty predator nearby.

She felt the beast thrash, she knew it had a hold on her sightless attacker. As she turned to watch the water roil behind her, she saw the old boat bobbing nearby. She struck out around the area of bubbling water, praying that the animal was so busy with his current meal that it wouldn't have time to come for her.

She couldn't feel her arms anymore; she couldn't feel any pain, any weakness. She couldn't feel anything but her adrenaline urging her to pull faster, kick harder, to reach the boat before she was pulled under. She was on the verge of tears as she grabbed the bottom rung of the boat ladder. She felt something powerful swim past her and she screamed. Andie willed her arms to pull her up and, mercifully, they did.

She quickly scrambled on to the boat deck. She looked down and could see the shark's fin moving back and forth, as the animal zigzagged, looking for the other bleeding creature it had sensed. She backed as far away from the side of the boat that she could, scared that somehow the predator would jump over the side and attack her.

Andie scrambled under the console; she crouched in a terrified ball of wet, bloody clothes and salt-soaked hair. She drew her knees up to her chest. She held her arms out in front of her and she started to cry. Andie tried to convince herself that she was safe now, that the man was dead, that the shark couldn't climb the ladder. But her fear wouldn't let go. She wrapped her arms around her legs and put her forehead on her knees. She cried with all of the fear in her life. She cried for Kallie. She cried for Frankie, her mother, and for Sean. She cried for Stacy in her loneliness, for Aphrodite and her disappointments on Broadway. She cried for Maria and her sick children.

Andie was so cocooned in the darkness of her fear that she did not hear the sirens of the coast guard boat. She did not see the flashing lights, or feel the hands that tried to urge her out of her hiding place. Andie was so deep inside of her own mind that she did not feel Sean wrap her lovingly in a blanket. She did not notice when he picked her up, cradling her like a child, and moved her to safety. It would be three days until she would learn that he stayed with her in the hospital all night that night, and that he only left at the insistence of her friends and family, so that he could eat and shower. It would be three days before she spoke a word about the events on the boat, to anyone.

Three Months Later

The jasmine was just beginning to bloom when Damian took Kallie out to celebrate 'The Winter Formal.' As Andie took pictures of them in front of the house, she breathed in the thick scent of the hidden vines. The night had been Damian's idea. Andie had told him about Kallie's beautiful dress, which hung in her room without hope of an occasion for it to be displayed properly. After that, the young medic concocted a plan to help her celebrate. With Andie's help, he reserved the deck at The Cabana on the Saturday night of the school dance, and he and Kallie enjoyed a romantic evening by the beach. He even rented a tuxedo.

"He looks awesome," Stacy said from where they watched through the sliding glass door.

Andie smiled and nodded as tears rolled down her face. She noticed how handsome Damian looked, sure, but really, she was crying over how beautiful her daughter was. She watched Kallie smile, watched as she threw her head back in a moment of unabashed laughter, as she danced slowly under the stars.

"She helped me survive," Andie finally said. "I just kept thinking about her, about not getting to see her in this dress." She turned and pulled Stacy back to the small table where they were enjoying appetizers while spying on the young couple.

"I bet she did, honey," Stacy reached over and rubbed her arm. She pulled back and clasped her hands together before she bowed her head and said in an uncharacteristically quiet voice, "Andie, I am so sorry. If I-"

Andie cut her off. "I've told you, this was not your fault."

"But if I had been there-"

"If you had been there he might have hurt you too, or he just would have come back and tried another time. Sean says I was the only one alive who could positively identify him. Given the string of bodies he left behind him I'm sure he wouldn't have stopped until I was dead, too."

"I know all of that, I mean... I know in my head, but my heart has a big bleeding spot that opened when I thought that I might never see you again."

It was Andie's turn to reach over and comfort her friend. "I totally understand that. I would feel the same way if something happened to you."

Andie thought back to the newspaper article from the week after her abduction:

Cursed Treasure Found at the Bottom of a Well.

As even the police did not have the full story, the press had to put together some of the pieces themselves. No one but Andie was still alive to fill in the blanks. As far as anyone could tell, two men had gone camping on private land, where they stumbled on the old well. Andie could imagine their surprise when they pulled up Spanish doubloons. At least one of them was a technical diver, so he must have known what they needed to do in order to retrieve the rest of the treasure. Either they knew Cowboy Sink was there, or they went looking for it, and that's when they required the help of at least one more trained cave diver. Even greed couldn't get a good technical diver into an unknown system of caves alone.

It appeared that when one of the divers died trying to retrieve the treasure, the remaining men let the desire for fortune get the better of them. The initial death was ruled an accident by both Stacy and the IUR&R, but reporting the death surely would have opened up the treasure site to federal and state investigation, and the divers would have lost the artifacts to the rightful owner of the property. Maybe one of the men felt bad and wanted to go to the police, or maybe there was a fight about the gold, but either way, one by one, the members of the treasure hunting crew started to die horrifying deaths.

Maybe the treasure actually was cursed, Andie thought.

She could only guess that after Ross and Tony died, Frankie got antsy. It didn't surprise Andie that the Skinny Man who kidnapped her was willing to get rid of him, too.

Andie turned her attention back to the couple on the deck.

"She's amazing, Andie. You did good," Stacy eventually said.

Andie smiled and nodded.

"And he's not bad either," Stacy continued.

"*Then ntrepesae inemoro!* He could be your son! Will you cut it out? Get a steady sweetheart already, okay?"

"I like it this way," Stacy said seriously. "I like the freedom, and I like the temporary companionship. I like pretty things and sex, and that's ok. It's taken me a while to get to this place, to get over the restrictive morals of my childhood, but I'm happy, trust me. Speaking of happy... Is Sean still being super protective of you?"

"He's let up a little bit. Since I started taking self-defense classes and managed to floor him one night, he seems to feel better about letting me out of his sight."

"You 'floored' him huh? How was that...?" Stacy smiled slyly.

Andie just rolled her eyes and kept watching Kallie and Damian. The thought of never seeing Kallie again drifted back into her mind. Ever since that night on the boat, Andie's mind had been like a cat toy, where the pet pushes the ball around and around in a never-ending circle. Only Andie couldn't just put her hand down and stop the maddening repetition. She had to follow the circle through each time. Any reminder would trigger it, and she would run through the whole night: the gratitude that Kallie had gone out and was not home when the man came; the blow to her head; the smells. Then Frankie's dead face. That lingered like a negative image after looking directly at the sun. She felt the water in her throat, and then her skin crawled as she remembered the feeling of the shark brushing past her. She felt her muscles burn, and then she cried as the memory of thinking she would never see Kallie again forced its way in to her mind.

Her face fell and tears filled her eyes again.

"Oh honey, I was just kidding, you know that, right?" Stacy said apologetically.

"I tore a man's eyes out Stacy. Like, dug in and ripped out his globes."

"Which I, personally, think is awesome," Stacy added. She picked up her neon blue beverage and sipped on it as she eyed a young man at the bar.

Andie followed her line of vision. "Go," she said as she wiped her eyes with a napkin. "You've been ogling him since we got here. Seriously though, be safe, use a-."

"I know, use a condom, and don't go to his house. And I'll call you to let you know I'm home safe." Stacy winked. She stopped and kissed Andie, "You're safe now, Mama. Your daughter is happy, you're happy, I'm happy." She straightened up.

"See you tomorrow?" Andie asked.

"You know it," Stacy replied as she walked to the bar. She angled herself in sidewise next to the buff tourist in a lifeguard tank top.

Andie's phone rang and a smiling picture of Sean flashed on the screen.

"Hey, Detective Malone, how are you?" she answered.

"Better now that I'm talking to you," he responded. She heard the smile in his voice.

"Awww, thanks." Hearing him talk soothed her. His deep, calming voice momentarily stood in the way of the ever-revolving cat toy.

"How's it going?" he asked.

Andie stared through the glass again. She watched as Kallie and Damian turned in a slow circle, swaying gently to whatever song was playing.

"I like him," she answered. "And Kallie looks deliriously happy. I think it's going well."

"Is Stacy still there?"

Andie looked over at the bar. Stacy was bent in close to the drunken young man. "Not for long," she responded with a chuckle. "Are you going to be able to make it? I would love to dance with you next to the ocean."

"I'm trying to finish up, but I'm not sure if I'll be done in time, I'm sorry, babe."

Andie thought of pouting; her instinct was to pull out a guilt-producing line about being alone. But she didn't. Just as Stacy had, Andie was practicing new behavior, trying to break the habits learned as a child.

"No worries," she finally said. "Take care of what you need to do. I just request some of your time tomorrow, if that's ok."

"How about a walk on the beach at sunset?" Sean asked.

"That sounds amazing. I'll call you after church."

"And remember, we have that thing on Tuesday, the unveiling of the treasure at the museum in Tampa," Sean added. "I saw the exhibit, they did a really nice job. Someone wrote a whole bit on the dagger, saying it was cursed. It's got its own folklore now. The press'll be there too, so be ready to have your picture taken."

"I'm going to have to agree with the cursed theory. Regardless of how that knife ended up at the bottom of the well, it certainly didn't have a very auspicious reintroduction to the world." Andie recalled the image of her patient, twisted in his final agonizing moments of life. "And the press will be more interested in what you have to say, about the investigation, the murders, and the treasure. No one will pay much attention to me."

"Are you kidding? Not only are you the most beautiful woman who ever lived, you also were the only person involved in this whole mess to survive. Of course they'll pay attention to you."

Andie fingered the scar on the back of her head. Her memories of the time after the abduction were still blurry. After she got out of the hospital, she had given an interview to the local press, but outside of that she only shared what details she could remember with the police and her close friends. Not even Sophia knew the extent of the experience. Andie didn't think she could handle it.

"I guess I just hope they won't pay attention to me," she responded, more to herself than to Sean. Andie gazed out at Kallie and Damian and wished the events six months ago had never happened. Sean didn't respond right away.

"Babe, it's all going to be ok. Call me tomorrow, ok?" he said. His voice was calming, and Andie believed him.

"Of course."

As she put the phone back down on the table, she watched the two young people share a slice of key lime pie on the deck. She reached up and touched the scar at the base of her skull again.

Stacy walked to her with the drunken tourist in tow.

"Good night, my love," she said. She kissed Andie on the head. "I'll see you tomorrow."

"Ok," Andie replied. As the pair walked away, she called, "You know my number if you need me." Without looking back, Stacy raised her drink in acknowledgement.

"Mom?!"

Kallie's voice surprised Andie and as she whirled around, she knocked over her water glass. Damian grabbed a pile of napkins from a nearby table.

"Hi, Dr. Markos," he smiled at her from the ground, where he was picking up the spilled ice cubes.

"Are you spying on me, Mom?" Kallie asked. Andie saw herself in her daughter, who had a hip out to one side and a hand resting accusatorily on her hipbone.

"Yes, yes I am," Andie answered. She stood up and embraced Kallie. "Deal with it kid. I love you too much to let you go this easily."

Kallie slowly put her arms around Andie's waist and hugged her back.

"I love you, too, Mom."

About Isabella Adams

Isabella (Izzy) lives in a small town on the Gulf Coast of Florida with her husband, three children, and her golden retriever, Isaac. She spends her days working as a health care professional, and her evenings with her family and her writing. Homework, dance classes, dinner, and too much laundry to imagine, mean that Izzy enjoys a full, rich life. She brings those experiences to her work, her writing, and to her daily approach to life's gifts and challenges.

Social Media Links

Website: https://www.izzyadams.com/

Twitter: https://twitter.com/izzybellaadams
@izzybellaadams

Acknowledgements

Many people have been instrumental in the evolution of this story. First, I would like to extend my gratitude to Aphrodite and Kallie. They are both indispensable and irreplaceable in my real world, everyday life.

I would also like to thank my best friend, Laura, for her continuous support and assistance. The most important thing, however, is her unwavering ability to laugh with me about my crashing of Microsoft Word's spell checker. Thanks for being with me every step of the way.

A huge thank you goes to my husband, FF Amanti, for his wealth of knowledge about technical diving. Without his stories, I never would have had the inspiration necessary to bring the cave world to life.

Lastly, I need to thank Missy, who has supported me and listened when I needed it, and Robyn, without whom I never would have made it this far in my job and my life. Thanks to both for their encouragement, input, and friendship.

Made in the USA
Columbia, SC
07 November 2017